"Why do you tease me so?" Amanda asked breathlessly.

Jesse studied her. "What makes you think I'm teasing?"

"Because I know who you are, Jess. I know *what* you are. You're a rounder and a renegade. The last thing you'd want is a woman like me."

"And what kind of woman is that? Tell me, but leave out what I already know." His gaze dropped to the skin revealed by her robe. "That you're a woman who wears sexy silk kimonos with nothing underneath. That you come midnight-calling in your bare feet. That you're a woman who responds to me."

"Stop it! It's a joke to you, isn't it? I'm the furthest thing from the women you're used to—I'm your basic plain Jane, no-nonsense Girl Scout type. I wasn't what you wanted ten years ago, and I'm not what you want now. Your exploits are legendary!"

"Who's been feeding you all these lies about me?" Jesse demanded. "Your father?"

"He has nothing to do with this!" she said fiercely. Amanda raised her hand to sock him one, but Jesse saw it coming. He grabbed her arm and pulled her up against him. Holding her so their mouths were all but touching, he forced her to look at him. "You think I didn't ache for you all those times you turned your brown eyes on me? Eyes that said, I want you? One of the most noble acts this outlaw ever committed was when I resisted the temptation of giving you your first taste of passion. You hated me for it then. I hated myself for not taking it."

Jess's voice lowered to a whisper. "Don't hate me now, Amanda. Give me what we've both waited ten long years for me to take. . . ."

WHAT ARE *LOVESWEPT* ROMANCES?

They are stories of true romance and touching emotion. We believe those two very important ingredients are constants in our highly sensual and very believable stories in the *LOVESWEPT* line. Our goal is to give you, the reader, stories of consistently high quality that may sometimes make you laugh, sometimes make you cry, but are always fresh and creative and contain many delightful surprises within their pages.

Most romance fans read an enormous number of books. Those they truly love, they keep. Others may be traded with friends and soon forgotten. We hope that each *LOVESWEPT* romance will be a treasure—a "keeper." We will always try to publish

LOVE STORIES YOU'LL NEVER FORGET
BY AUTHORS YOU'LL ALWAYS REMEMBER

The Editors

LOVESWEPT® · **484**

Cindy Gerard

Maverick

BANTAM BOOKS
NEW YORK · TORONTO · LONDON · SYDNEY · AUCKLAND

MAVERICK

A Bantam Book / July 1991

ISBN 0-553-44162-0

Thank you

Special thanks to my cheerleaders, Barb, Awesome, and Rosie who put up with the BAD and the UGLY, and to Debbie, who helped me get to the GOOD.

Mom and Dad, this one's for you.

One

One thing hadn't changed: The view from the hay-mow door. Amanda could see for miles, over the shimmering banks of evergreens bordering the ranch house to the gently sloping foothills dotted with cattle. Beyond was the Garnet Range of the Montana Rockies. Their jagged, purple peaks rose like towering sentinels to guard the lush Blackfoot River Valley far below.

No, she thought in silent awe, the view hadn't changed, but her status had. Once she'd been the hired man's daughter, and now—though at times she still had trouble believing it—she owned the ranch. A good chunk of it anyway.

Feeling both the pride and the strain of the day's labor, Amanda straightened and tried to work the kinks out of her back.

"Gettin' soft on me, darlin'?"

She grinned over her shoulder at Willie Brady. Her cagey old foreman tried to hide his knowing smile as he turned and lugged a fifty-pound hay bale to the top of the stack.

"Soft," Amanda said, "is what I was three months

ago when I moved back here. Tired is what I am today. Just like you are." She tugged off a work-worn glove and scowled at the angry red welts on her palm. "For this, I gave up coffee breaks, paid vacations, and as many cases of acid indigestion as I could pack into a week of deadlines."

Willie chuckled. "Did I hear a little cry of 'uncle' in there somewhere, boss?"

"When pigs fly." Amanda's theft of one of Willie's favorite phrases earned an indignant snort from him.

She laughed as she drew the glove back on. She and Willie both knew it would take nothing short of a nuclear holocaust to blast her back to Bozeman, Montana. If she hadn't folded under the strain of several mysterious accidents that had plagued the ranch the past month, it wasn't likely she'd be packing it in now.

Besides, someone had already filled the lucrative position she'd held for four years as a computer programmer for Montana Life. Whoever it was, he or she was welcome to it. Now that she was out from under the stress and confinement of the city and back under the Big Sky where she belonged, Amanda Carter wasn't going anywhere. She was home, and home she'd stay.

"If you had as much muscle as you have stubbornness," Willie grumbled around the toothpick he perpetually nursed in the corner of his mouth, "it wouldn't be so bad. Why, drippin' wet from a dunkin' in the horse tank, you couldn't tip a scale much over a hundred pounds. And what's more," he continued, giving the brim of his hat a fierce tug, "you damn near can't see over the back of that rank old stallion you call a mount. A little bit of a thing like you's got no business workin' like a man."

Amanda groaned as she flipped her long blonde

braid back over her shoulder and reached for another bale. It was an old argument between them. When she'd shown up in her blue jeans and boots that chilly March morning three months ago, Willie had voiced his opinion of her with a heavy dose of hostility. Today, only affection came through.

"You don't really want to fight, do you, Willie?" she asked, glancing at him.

"Don't you go snappin' those black eyes at me, Mandy Carter. I call 'em like I see 'em, and I see this as man's work. I know, I know." One bony hand held off her protest with a patronizing pat of the air. "You can tote a bale with the best of 'em. Now, ain't you proud?"

She pointedly ignored his sarcasm. "Let's just get this over with, okay? A couple more loads and we'll call it a day."

A movement on the road far below caught her attention as she turned back toward the conveyer. An approaching car kicked up a snaking trail of gravel dust on its reckless trip toward the main house. Leaning out the mow door, Amanda shaded her eyes against the sun's glare to get a better look.

"Looks like we've got company," she said, frowning.

Willie shuffled up behind her. He glanced down at the road and let out an interested snort. Snorting was one of Willie's favorite ways of expressing himself. He'd honed the practice to a fine art.

"*We* don't got nothin'," he said dryly as the toothpick slid from one side of his mouth to the other. "*You* got it. And what you got ain't company. It's trouble . . . as if you needed more of that. Damned if it ain't your partner, honey. You've been waiting for the day of reckoning. Looks like it's finally here."

Amanda took a closer look, then recognized the car. She'd seen Jesse Kincannon's Porsche only once, at the lawyer's office when Walt Kincannon's will had been read, back in February. She'd known since then that this confrontation with Walt's son was inevitable. She'd known, but she had hoped she would have time to prepare for it.

When she'd played this scene in her mind, her hair and makeup had been perfect, her clothes sophisticated. She'd planned to face Jesse Kincannon in soft wool or watery silk, not wash-faded flannel and bleached-out denim. And she certainly hadn't pictured herself in a Becky Thatcher braid full of hay chaff and a sweat-streaked layer of road dust coating her face.

That same road dust settled like a pale mist over Jesse's sleek black Porsche as it skidded to a stop in the middle of the drive. As its driver shoved open the door, Amanda fought to ignore the buzz of unwanted excitement that scuttled through her body. She watched in edgy silence as one long, lean blue-jean clad leg settled a Tony Lama boot onto the gravel. The leg was joined by its mate, then by a whole lot of arrogant, dark-haired male as Jesse Kincannon eased his six-foot-plus frame out of the low-slung sports car.

Amanda's heart kicked into a Montana two-step.

Willie was right, she thought, swearing softly under her breath. The last thing she needed right now was another problem. Jesse Kincannon was definitely that. He always had been.

Well, she told herself, you could pick your friends, but not your problems. Even so, an even break wouldn't have hurt. Resigned to face the music, she drew in a deep, fortifying breath. "I wondered when he'd get around to showing up."

"You don't have to wonder no more," Willie said matter-of-factly. "And you don't have to wear that hangdog look neither. You can hold your own with a maverick like him. Him and his sister, too, if you have to."

Amanda gave a smile full of affection to the man who had replaced her father as foreman, when a bad hip had forced Les Carter to retire ten years ago. In the few short months since she'd moved back to the Flying K and taken over its management, Willie had expanded his role even more. He'd become like family to her. And already he could read her too well. Her futile attempt to appear unaffected by Jesse's arrival hadn't fooled him for a second. "You're a very nice person, Mr. Brady, do you know that?"

Willie's leathery face turned beet-red beneath his seasoned tan. He tugged the dog-eared brim of his battered Stetson lower on his forehead. "Just don't spread it around. I'd never be able to keep your hired hands in line if they suspected."

Amanda smiled. "Don't worry, Willie. They don't suspect. They all know."

Growing serious, Willie took her small hand in his own rough, callused hand. With uncharacteristic directness, he looked her straight in the eye. "Try to keep something in mind when you're dealing with Jesse. His pa was as good as they get. Now, I know them two had problems right from the get-go, but I figure there's bound to be some of the old man in the boy somewhere . . . even if it don't appear to be fightin' to get out."

"Jesse Kincannon has never had to fight for anything in his life," Amanda said tightly. "I seriously doubt he'll start fighting now. He probably figures he can waltz right in, take what he came for, then go on about his business."

"And what do you suppose he came for, girl?"

"No big secret there." She drew in a deep breath. "He came to get back what is now my half of the Flying K. Once he finds out I'm not leaving, and that

I'm not willing to sell to the land developers gobbling up the Valley, he'll head out of here so fast, we'll wonder if we just imagined he showed up."

"Assuming that's why he's here, what makes you figure he'd give up so easy?"

Unaware of the gesture, Amanda gave a good imitation of Willie's indignant snort. "Would he want to squirrel himself away out here on this isolated ranch? Uh-uh. Unless he's changed a whole hell of a lot, the Flying K is definitely not his style. From what I hear, he's as happy as a bull in sweet clover right now and doesn't have a thimbleful of thoughts about giving up his ways."

Willie narrowed his eyes thoughtfully, then took the plunge. "What exactly do you hear?"

Amanda stared down at Jesse. He was leaning against the hood of the car, taking in his surroundings with a slow, thorough gaze. With the flashy good looks to match his sleek, sexy Porsche, he should have looked as out of place on a working cattle ranch as a hay wagon would look rumbling down Park Avenue. He didn't. Instead, he looked for all the world like a man who'd just realized he'd been away too long.

Brushing aside that unsettling observation, Amanda slapped the dust off the thighs of her faded jeans and headed for the haymow ladder.

"I hear the same things you do, Willie," she said with a scowl. "He's still the stereotypical poor little rich man's child. He's reckless, roguish, all flash and freewheeling fun. Word is, he's never done an honest day's work since he left here and he feeds off women like a piranha feeds off fresh meat."

Willie whistled low and long. "That's not the most generous picture I've ever seen painted."

"Maybe not, but I'll bet it's not far from the mark. He's no good, Willie, and you know it."

"I remember the day, many moons ago, when you thought he could walk on water and make it rain."

Amanda cast off that piece of ancient history with a defensive tilt of her chin. "I was a kid. He was the boss's son. Besides, it didn't take me long to figure out what he was after. The only thing I *don't* have figured out is what took him so long to show up and how much trouble he's going to give me before he gets bored and leaves."

"What makes you so sure he's here to give you grief?"

Amanda paused on the first rung of the ladder, the slightest hint of a grin on her face. "The same thing that makes me sure that every morning when you get up, you're going to pull on those worn-out pieces of leather you call boots, down a mug of scalding mud-thick brew you refer to as coffee, then start giving me guff about why I shouldn't be workin' like a man.

"Leopards don't change their spots, Willie. And skunks like Jesse Kincannon don't lose their scent. From the time he was old enough to figure out he could rile me, he used every conceivable way he knew to do it. I don't see him breaking the pattern, especially not when there's something as big as the ranch at stake."

"Sounds to me like the man gets under your skin."

She shook her head firmly. "The man *got* under my skin," she called as she scaled down the narrow wooden ladder. "Past tense. Except for our meeting at Walt's lawyers, I haven't seen Jesse in almost ten years. I've changed. I'm not the same malleable little girl who used to trip over herself trying to please the boss man's son." And she was mature enough to handle him now, she added with silent conviction as she hit the barn floor.

Yet for all her determination, Amanda was having difficulty dismissing the low tingling in her belly simply as a nervous reaction to the coming confrontation. Come on, Carter, she told herself. She was way past sixteen. Way past reacting to Jesse Kincannon like an inquisitive virgin quaking to experience her first kiss.

But it was there, sexual awareness, humming through her senses, weakening her knees. It was overrated, overblown, and the last thing she needed when she faced Jesse.

Disgusted by the feelings, Amanda smoothed a hand over her hair and looked up the ladder at Willie. "Are you coming?" she asked.

Willie thumbed back his hat and shook his head. "Don't sound to me like I'm needed. Since you seem to think you got the boy all figured out, I'll just finish up here while you go see what he wants."

What Jesse Kincannon wanted was a good, long look at Amanda Carter. He'd waited more than three months to get it. As he watched her stride toward him, her gait confident and sure, her slim legs sexy as hell in those soft faded jeans, he decided the wait had been worth it. The Amanda Carter he'd seen in Ed Dillman's law office three months earlier had been no illusion. Yes, indeed, he thought. Carter's little pill had grown into a woman.

When she stopped a few feet away from him, he folded his arms loosely across his chest and got more comfortable against the hood of the Porsche. Taking his sweet time, he made a lengthy assessment of her willow thin, yet softly feminine figure. He found great pleasure in the earthy, dust-streaked, and disheveled look of her, and even greater pleasure in the pretty blush that flooded her cheeks.

"Hello, Amanda," he said finally and without a trace of apology for his bold and brazen stare.

She squared her shoulders, making an obvious and valiant effort to retain her composure. "Jesse." Nodding curtly, she extended a small, slim hand.

Jesse took it and held it, feeling both her delicacy and a faint trembling just beneath the surface. He let a slow, pleased smile creep over his face. She didn't want to, but she reacted to him. He hadn't been sure she would. The calm, collected businesswoman he'd faced over the conference table last February had been as cool and distant as an iceberg. She'd listened to the reading of his father's will with controlled detachment, as if she'd known what neither he nor his sister had known. As if she'd expected to hear that Walt had left half interest in the Flying K to his old foreman's daughter.

She tugged her hand away from his grasp. He let go with considerable reluctance.

"You should have let me know you were coming," she said, hastily tucking both hands into her hip pockets. "I'd have had Tina put together something special for dinner. Unless, of course, you can't stay that long."

Jesse almost laughed. She hadn't said it, but her inflection clearly suggested that she hoped he'd make a beeline right back down the drive.

"Don't worry about dinner tonight." He walked around the car, opened the trunk, and tugged out a pair of well-used and well-stuffed suitcases. "Tina will have plenty of other opportunities to show off her special talents. Does she still make the meanest chili this side of the Rockies?"

He did laugh then, at the way Amanda's face paled. At the stunned look in her eyes as she stared at his luggage.

"Careful, Sunshine," he said. "Your disappointment is showing."

Her quick attempt at recovery was just that—an attempt. "You're staying?"

He nodded, still grinning. She had nothing to say to that, and it tickled the hell out of him. She just turned and started to walk away, leaving him to watch her trim little backside.

It was a backside worth watching. It always had been. So was the subtle hip action that went with it. Ten years had added new dimension to the curves beneath the well-worn jeans, but she'd made him pant even as a teenager. His little "Sunshine" had never failed to make him hot. He smiled, remembering.

That last summer he'd been home, she'd been sixteen to his twenty, and she'd been temptation with a capital T. Jailbait. Though he'd made his interest crystal and sometimes leeringly clear, Amanda, in her innocence, hadn't had an inkling of the rabble she roused in him. Every time he'd watched her walk by, she'd been in danger of losing that sweet virginity she'd guarded so well and he'd fantasized about stealing. While he would plead guilty to seducing a few steamy kisses out of her, he had, with great difficulty and no lack of pain, backed off before it was too late. Not taking advantage of her inexperience was one of the few good things he'd done back then. He smiled and gave credit where credit was due. Her daddy's shotgun had definitely been influential.

Realizing that he hadn't moved away from the car, Jesse snagged a bag in each hand and followed her toward the main house. He wondered which bedroom she'd chosen for herself. He could picture her in the blue room . . . in the big four-poster . . . on cool white percale and delicate eyelet lace.

"I'll just open things up for you," she said when he caught up with her, sounding and looking like a dutiful hostess as she marched, eyes forward, fixed on the front door. "The house is bound to smell a little musty after being closed up for so long."

"Closed up?"

"Except for the kitchen. Tina still prepares the men's meals there."

"Why haven't you moved in yet?"

She didn't look at him. "I'm not moving in."

Somehow, he wasn't surprised. He was curious, though. When she glanced at him, his eyes must have telegraphed his question.

"I grew up in the foreman's cottage," she explained evenly. "I'm comfortable living there."

It was the look in her dark eyes, as much as her words that said, "end of discussion." Giving her the room she seemed to think she needed, he backed off and followed slowly behind.

Considering her defensiveness and her cold shoulder, he wondered how long it would take for her to mention the trouble she'd been having with the ranch.

And considering the memories and the high-voltage, sensual energy he felt shuttling between them, he wondered how long it would take him to get her into that big old four-poster.

Two

Damn his devil eyes! Amanda thought. They should be black like his hair, not blue like the sky. They should be menacing, not mesmerizing. And they should be hating her, not haunting her. Like now. She should be sleeping. She was wide awake. Thinking of him. Aching for him. Him and his damn devil eyes.

She punched her pillow and flattened it over her ears. She didn't want to hear the soft strains of Jesse's guitar floating in through her open bedroom window. Who did he think he was, George Strait? And why were the notes he coaxed from that battered old box so sultry and slow, his lyrics so honeyed and captivating? A trace of the South flavored his already-seductive voice. Like a hot summer wind it drifted over her senses in a sweet, sensual caress. She shivered despite the heat and hugged her pillow tighter.

He'd been there all of a week now and wasn't showing the tiniest inclination to leave. In fact, he seemed to be enjoying himself. She never would have guessed it. He donned work boots and denims each morning, worked alongside the men all day, and sat his big bay gelding with an unsettling amount of authority. Then he had the nerve to drive her crazy each night when he relaxed outside on the patio, tormenting her with his love songs. Not that he was singing to her. Not that she wanted him to . . .

Flipping angrily onto her stomach, Amanda buried her face in the mattress. He was a smooth one all right. He'd even fooled Willie, had her wily old foreman eating out of the palm of his hand. From the moment Willie had found him in the barn that first morning, things had gone from bad to worse.

"I tell you, Amanda," Willie had said with a laugh, "the man was ankle-deep in horse manure, muckin' out a stall. There he stood in a pair of grungy old jeans and a *Life's a Beach* T-shirt, grinnin' as if he had good sense. You got to admit, Mandy-girl, a man who ain't afraid of hard, dirty work can't be all bad."

Amanda snarled into her pillow. Even the ranch hands treated him like the long lost son who'd arrived to save the family fortune, not the black sheep returned to raid and plunder. It had taken her the better part of two months to get those men to respect her, and she had a sneaking suspicion that if it weren't for Willie's endorsement, they'd still be treating her as odd man out. To this day, Smiling Jake Slater glared at her like she was pure poison.

Sighing, Amanda wrestled with the sheets until she'd rolled onto her back, then lay staring into the darkness toward the ceiling.

She didn't want to, but she had to give Jesse credit. He didn't interfere, and not once had he pressured her to sell. Grudgingly, she admired him for that. After all, he and his sister, Lucy, owned fifty percent of the ranch. Fifty percent of a thirty-thousand-acre operation was no small interest.

Still, as far as Amanda was concerned, the only real

good to come from Jesse's unannounced visit was that the "accidents" had stopped. From the beginning she'd wanted to chalk them up to coincidence, anyway, even though Willie had fretted and fussed like a setting hen. But now that Jesse was there and things had quieted down, she was beginning to wonder. And Jesse was being entirely too agreeable. He *had* to be up to something.

With a frustrated growl, Amanda gave up any hope of sleep. She flung her pillow to the floor, then whipped back her tangled sheets and snatched her thigh-length kimono from the hook on her bedroom door. Wrapping the blue silk tightly around her, she marched through the kitchen and out the back door with every intention of confronting him.

The ranch house was only a stone's throw from her little cottage. Even so, she'd lost the head off her steam by the time she neared the rambling structure and spotted Jesse on the patio. She came to a halt and to her senses at the same mind-clearing instant, when it occurred to her what she was wearing beneath the kimono. Exactly nothing.

The night grass was dewy wet and springtime cool beneath her bare feet as she stood still, her heart pounding. What had she thought she was going to say when she confronted him anyway? she asked herself, shifting from one cold foot to the other. But as she watched Jesse from the cover of the lilacs, she forgot her purpose and her lack of attire altogether and just stared.

His face was cast in half-shadow by the pale light of a full butter-yellow moon. It was a renegade moon. A night made for raiding. Jesse had a renegade smile. The two went hand in hand.

He was sprawled comfortably in a lawn chair, totally unaware of her presence. His hair was still damp from a late shower, and though he'd taken the time to pull on a clean work shirt, he'd left it negligently open, not bothering to tuck the tails into his jeans. His old guitar was cradled snugly against his lean belly, his ankles were crossed, and his bare feet were propped on the patio table. A half-full tumbler of iced whiskey sat on the table within easy reach.

He was the picture of lazy, sensual contentment as he strummed a plaintive melody, sometimes singing the haunting refrain, sometimes humming softly. Watching him, listening to him, Amanda felt something inside her melt, drizzling through all her erogenous zones and pooling like warm butter in the lowest part of her belly.

What was it about him that had always made her blood run thick and heavy, her heartbeat clumsy and quick? It wasn't as if she were inexperienced. At twenty-six, she hadn't exactly been around the block with the big girls, but she'd had relationships. Well, one relationship. So it hadn't been successful. So it hadn't been sweet. Just because she'd sworn off men for a while because of it didn't mean she was sexually frustrated.

Okay! she admitted, shifting to her other foot again. She was sexually frustrated. That might be part of her problem, but Jesse Kincannon certainly wasn't the cure. Somehow, she had to come to terms with this unprecedented and unreasonable fascination with him, which was probably just an adolescent carryover from that summer, oh, so many years ago.

She'd thought she loved him then, but right now she didn't much like him. Yet from the moment she'd watched him unfold himself from his sleek, sexy car, which so exemplified its driver, she'd known she was in trouble. What woman with a healthy libido wouldn't be? If a toned, agile build hung on a six-feet-three-inch frame wasn't enough to stir her interest, his rakish good looks and outlaw grin were the final hook.

She'd been a child of sixteen when he'd first had that effect on her. She was a woman now. A knot of sheer feminine desire curled tighter inside her as she studied the bold lines of his face through a woman's eyes.

His solid, square jaw presented a complete and total incongruity to the fluid mobility of his thick black hair and wide, expressive mouth . . . a mouth whose corners seemed perpetually tipped up in a fascinating yet infuriating semblance of a grin. The only distinction between a sneer of superiority, a grin of benign innocence, or a warm smile of sincere and utter benevolence, was whatever expression she found in his eyes.

Blue as a Montana sky at morning, liquid as a clear mountain stream, his eyes had been spawned by the devil to deliver temptation. And Jesse Kincannon delivered that temptation with an ease that defied description. Amanda shivered in the wake of over-heated blood sluicing through her veins, then cursed the weakness in her character that made her susceptible to the biologic masterpiece and throwaway charm that was Jesse Kincannon. She had little doubt he'd left a path of vanquished women from Montana to Maine. Only a fool would let herself become one more casualty along the route. Self-defense finally prompted her to begin inching back toward her cottage before she embarrassed herself.

Her rustling movement quieted Jesse's guitar and brought his head up. Amanda froze as his gaze searched the darkness beyond the lilac bushes. When he grinned broadly and struck up a bluesy rendition of "You Are My Sunshine," she knew she'd been found out.

Against all reason, she smiled, then considered her

predicament. if she turned now and ran, she'd only look more ridiculous. Sighing with defeat, she knotted the silk belt tighter and stepped out of the deepest part of the shadows.

He stopped his strumming and cocked his dark head to the side when she entered his line of sight. "Never figured you for a window peeper, Sunshine," he drawled, "but to each his own, I always say."

Some people, she thought, might find his particular I'm-full-of-myself look attractive. There was no mistaking its invitation. His eyes said, "anytime you're ready, sweetheart," and his smile—sneer, smirk, whatever—restated that invitation every time their paths crossed. Damn him, if he didn't say it again tonight. Oh, he was something, this fast-lane drifter who was dabbling at playing Wrangler Dan.

Irritated that he could so easily get to her, she bit out a question. "Why have you always called me that?"

"Sunshine?" he asked with a speculative arch of a dark eyebrow. "Because that's what you are. All that sunflower-yellow hair, that bright toothpaste-ad smile, that sweet-as-honey disposition. It all adds up to sunshine . . . Sunshine."

Rattled by the uncharacteristic note of affection threaded through his totally characteristic sensual delivery, she blurted out the first thing that came to mind. "I didn't see much of you today."

"So you decided to watch me from the bushes tonight?" He laughed at her scowl, then added, "I had a little errand to run this afternoon." Apparently unable to resist, he grinned and asked, "Did you miss me?"

She *had* missed him. It made her mad as hell to admit it even to herself, and she'd be damned if she'd admit it to him. Before she made a bigger fool of herself, she turned to go.

"You have wise eyes, did you know that, Amanda?"

His whiskey-rough voice brought her head around and set her heart racing. His expression had transformed from playful to pensive and, if she could believe it, sincere.

"Even when you were a little girl," he went on, "playing Annie Oakley to my Billy the Kid, you had the ability to make me stop and wonder if you really knew as much as your eyes said you did. Pretty brown-eyed Amanda." His sultry blue eyes searched her own. "I've thought about you a lot over the years. Have you thought about me?"

He's teasing you, Amanda, she told herself. Don't let him take you in. Impatient with his soft words and her body's reaction to their implication, she asked what most needed asking. "Why are you here, Jess?"

His gaze searched hers across the darkness before he cocked his head to the side, considering her question. "Restless, I guess," he answered finally. "Couldn't sleep. The night air is peaceful. Thought a little dose of it and a few bars of Willie and the boys would help me unwind."

Amanda swallowed back her own restlessness. "Don't play with me, Jess. You know what I'm asking. What are you doing here at the Flying K?"

"If you come over here and out of the dark, I'll tell you."

It was a challenge, plain and simple, and one she couldn't turn away from. Excruciatingly aware of her nakedness beneath the thin silk robe, she walked haltingly across the tiled patio. She stopped just out of reach and stood with the table between them. Jesse welcomed her with yet another grin, the one, she thought ruefully, he most regularly and annoyingly used on her. It gave her the distinct impression that he knew exactly the effect he had on her.

To combat it, she tried to focus on his feet, but

even their broad, bare soles emanated virility. Her stomach rose and fell like a fast-moving elevator, and she dragged her gaze to his face. What she saw made her breath catch.

His lazy smile had faded. His eyes glittered darkly as he made a slow, utterly carnal sweep of her, from the tips of her cold toes to where her kimono met the bare skin of her upper thighs, then on to her unbound breasts. To her horror, Amanda felt her nipples harden and press against the thin silk.

The heavy silence went on for too long. "The truth, Jess," she finally managed to say. "Why are you here?"

He tore his gaze away from her breasts and closed his eyes, drawing in a long, deep breath.

"Well," he said, plucking absently at the steel strings, then silencing them with the flat of his hand, "it's about damn time."

Setting the guitar on the tile beside his chair, he sat forward and met her eyes. "You've been pussyfooting around me like a skittish mare dodging a randy stallion. I was wondering when you'd get around to asking. But tell me first, what finally brought about your curiosity tonight?"

Feeling exposed and unsure of herself, Amanda shrugged. "I guess skittish goes against the grain. There comes a time when straightforward and direct is the best course of action."

"I agree," he said softly.

"So, it's back to square one," she said, fighting the temptation of his eyes. "Why did you come to the Flying K? Or better yet, why didn't you show up sooner?"

His shrug mimicked her earlier one. "I came because I missed the place. Specifically the quiet, the simplicity, the mountains. You." He paused and waited for that little bomb to settle before continuing. "I didn't come sooner because I couldn't get away. And because I knew Walt had left things in good hands."

Amanda chewed on that for a while, then asked, "No animosity? No 'you're not entitled to half of the ranch and I fully intend to see that the will is declared null and void'?"

He shook his head. "Not my style."

A week ago, Amanda had been certain she had an accurate accounting of what his style was. Now she wasn't so sure. "It's your sister's style," she said. "Your sister's words, actually."

"I remember. She wasn't too nice to you at the reading of the will, was she? Don't worry. Lucy's a lot of smoke and little fire. She'll cool down when she sees you're an adept manager."

"Then you know about the threats she's been making?"

A frown deepened the V between his brows. "Threats?"

Clearly, he didn't know, Amanda mused. Or at least, he wanted her to think as much. "She calls regularly. I get letters once a week. In the last one, she accused me of seducing Walt." Amanda hugged her arms around her waist and shivered in disgust. "To date, she's called me a gold digger, an opportunist, and a manipulator. Those are some of her more delicate terms. She claims I took advantage of Walt during the last months of his illness. That I'd been meeting with him behind everyone's back and convinced him to change his will."

"Did you?" Jesse asked.

"Take advantage of him?" she snapped, flashing her own brand of fire.

"No, Sunshine." That smile snuck back again. "Walt Kincannon was too sharp, even in his old age, to let anyone use him. What I want to know is, did you seduce him? I'd rest easier knowing the old man died content."

Stunned, Amanda stared at his arrogant smirk for a breathless moment. Her anger wrapped tightly around her, insulating her from the effect of his laughing eyes. Relieved somehow that she'd finally uncovered what she'd known was lurking beneath his smooth surface all along, she answered his insult with one of her own. "You're a pig, you know that, Kincannon?"

He chuckled good-naturedly. "Don't go getting your back up. You seemed so determined to work up a good lather that I decided to help you vent a little. As tight-lipped and controlled as you've been around me this past week, I figured you deserved a good blowout to make you feel better. I was right, wasn't I?"

"Good night, Mr. Kincannon," she said with finality.

Before she could spin on her heel and beat an indignant retreat, Jesse shot out of his chair and latched onto her waist. Laughing at her anger, he tugged her around the table and onto his lap.

"Just like old times, huh?" he said, and laughed again, sending her into a flurry of activity. She fought his hands, but couldn't get up. She scrapped with everything that was in her to get away from him, while he just continued to laugh at her.

"Who the hell do you think you are?" she asked from between clenched teeth.

"Oh, for Pete's sake, settle down. You're more— Dammit, Amanda, will you . . . Amanda, knock it off! Ouch! You little wildcat! If you don't cool off and sit still . . . All right, you asked for it!"

In a lightning-quick move, he banded her wrists together behind her back. With his other hand, he stilled her thrashing legs. Falling against his chest exhausted, she blew a strand of hair from her mouth and glared at him.

"This is really silly, you know," he said between labored breaths.

She bucked hard in one last attempt to break free.

"Now, be still," he ordered hoarsely, sucking in a harsh breath. "Or I'm warning you, you're going to find yourself in more hot water than you've ever settled your cute little butt in before."

His threat finally got through to her. That and the fact that he'd overpowered her, easily. Her breathing was hard and fast. His, she noticed, wasn't much better. And he wasn't laughing anymore. She could feel the heavy rise and fall of his chest against her breasts. With all her twisting and thrashing, her hair was flying wildly around her face. Her robe hung disreputably open to her waist. The bottom hem was hiked up so high, there was nothing between her bare bottom and the solid, thick heat of him except his jeans.

Panicked and shamed by her helplessness, she threw back her head and stared fiercely at him. "Let me go."

Jesse let out his breath in a hiss, then met her eyes with unyielding intensity as he tightened his arm around her thighs. "Just—just give me a minute," he said in a ragged whisper. Closing his eyes, he drew in deep, shaky breaths.

Gradually, his breathing slowed. The arm slung around her legs loosened. Then his hand, broad, warm, and surprisingly rough with calluses, began a steady, almost-consoling caress up and down the length of her thigh.

"You all right?" he whispered finally, lowering his mouth to her hair.

All the fight deserted her. There was nothing left but embarrassment . . . of her childish tirade, of the thoroughly wanton way she was sprawled across his lap. Of her increasing awareness of his hard male body beneath her.

"Yes," she forced herself to say.

"Will you be good if I let go of your hands?" The low, gentle tone of his voice felt surprisingly comfortable. It matched the soothing sweep of his hand along her thigh.

She nodded against his chest, stirring to life the heated scent of his skin. It was musky and male and so totally dominated her senses, it was a moment before she realized he'd loosened his grip on her wrists.

As inconspicuously as possible, she drew the kimono closed over her breasts. It was Jesse, though, who tugged it down and covered her thighs.

Feeling utterly ridiculous, she lay still in his arms, unable to look at him. He matched her sigh with one of his own before giving in to a deep, rumbling chuckle.

"Well, now . . ." He wrapped both arms around her and hugged her quick and hard, then dropped a brotherly kiss on the top of her head. "Wasn't *that* fun? D'you learn all those moves bulldogging steers, or what?"

Amanda grudgingly let his good humor take over the mood. "Damn you, Jesse Kincannon," she said mildly. "You know good and well I learned those moves when I was sixteen years old and had to defend myself from you. You had problems with hormonal overload even then."

He gave her another affectionate squeeze, then released her. "Might be best if we leave my hormones out of this for a while. Unless, of course"—he paused, his look hopeful and full of sensual, mischievous invitation—"I'm reading you wrong."

She managed to manufacture a warning glare.

It did nothing to dampen his cocky grin. "I didn't think so."

Amanda sat up with as much dignity as she could muster and shifted her legs with the intent of climbing off his lap.

He stayed her much too easily . . . with a gentle hand on her hip and some left-handed reasoning that was all the more effective because it made absolutely no sense. "Stay," he said simply. "Sit with me like you used to. Remember?"

Oh, yes. She remembered and the memory shook her. He remembered too. She could almost see the picture reflected in his eyes of an eleven-year-old Jesse holding a seven-year-old Amanda on his lap as she showed him a butterfly or a frog or whatever had tripped the imagination of a child with a need to share.

"We'll talk," he said in response to her hesitant look. "I'll be good. You'll see. Just stay."

Reaching out, he tugged a strand of blonde hair away from the corner of her mouth. After tucking it behind her ear, he rested linked hands companionably over her thighs.

"Will we talk about what I want to talk about?" she asked.

"Anything you say." His drawl was honey-warm and full of persuasion as he grinned at her stubborn suspicion.

That drawl with its hint of the South would be a question for another time, she decided. Right now she needed answers to more important issues. "Are you ready to tell me what you're up to?"

"Why do I have to be up to something?" he asked, affecting an affronted scowl. "Why can't a man simply come home to rejuvenate and enjoy?"

"Most men could. But not you, Jess. You're a

drifter. Always have been. The truth this time. Why did you come back?"

He studied her thoughtfully. "I like the way you say my name. Jess. You've never called me that before. Always Jesse, like everyone else around here. Does that mean you think I've finally grown up?"

Amanda wanted to slap that smug look right off his face. She wanted to melt into a puddle at his feet. She *had* to get away from him. "Fine. Play it your way. I'm going to bed."

"Okay, okay," he said quickly, tugging her back onto his lap. "I came back because Willie called me."

"Willie?"

"He was concerned about the trouble you'd been having."

"Willie called you and asked you to come help find the source of the trouble?"

One corner of his mouth tipped up at that. "Actually, he called to accuse me of *being* the source of the trouble. He's very protective of you, you know. It appears he took up where your father left off. I had to scramble like hell to convince him that his phone call was the first I'd heard you were having problems. Which, by the way, brings me to my own bone of contention. I've been waiting for you to tell me about it. Willie says something's badly amiss around here."

"Willie is overreacting to a few unfortunate and purely coincidental accidents."

Jesse frowned. "Fences downed with wire-cutters, cattle disappearing in the middle of the night, toxic pollutants in the upper creek reservoir do not 'purely coincidental accidents' make. You've got a problem, Amanda, and you'd better face it."

She gave him a long look, then lifted her chin. "All right. Was Willie right? Are you my problem?"

Jesse gazed back at her, a bit sadly, she thought, and shook his head. "No, honey. I'm not your problem, and from what you've told me, I suppose the next direction your finger will point is toward Lucy."

Her silence was his answer.

"You'd be wrong, Amanda. I've already talked to her. Stopped over to see her on my way here last week. She doesn't know anything about it." At her doubtful expression, he added, "Come on, Amanda. I know Lucy's hot tempered, and I know she's resistant to the terms of Walt's will, but even she wouldn't be that mean."

Amanda would like to tell him she knew differently, that his sister was meaner than a she-bear with her paw in a trap. Walt Kincannon's daughter was as hard as the relentless Montana winters. Driven as a child and then as a woman to make her father proud, she'd been so aggressive, she'd scared away even the most ardent suitors. Now alone and middle-aged, Lucy Kincannon spent her days and nights alone in a small cottage in town, nurturing her hatred of Amanda. She'd become a bitter, vindictive woman. Jesse wouldn't want to hear any of that, Amanda was certain.

Accepting that fact, she tried another tack. "I guess that puts us back to my original notion that it's all purely coincidence. Nothing else makes sense. Except for you and Lucy, I haven't been back long enough to make any enemies."

"Let's get something straight, Amanda. You are not my enemy, nor are you Lucy's."

"It really doesn't bother you that your father left half the ranch to me? This is your home, Jess— Jesse," she corrected herself, uncomfortable now because of his comment. "It has to hurt. More than just a little."

He looked away. A muscle in his jaw worked hard before he turned back to her. "It was always more your home than mine, Amanda. You were born here, too, same as I was."

"But you're his son."

Jesse reached for his whiskey and took a long, slow sip. "I'm the son he never wanted, and you're the daughter of the man my father respected like a brother."

It was Amanda's turn to look away, away from the hurt he tried so hard to conceal, away from the guilt she couldn't help but feel. No one had ever needed to speculate why Walt and his only son hadn't gotten along. Jesse was a latecomer, an unexpected tag-along, more than ten years his sister's junior. His mother, not as strong as she should have been due to her age, had died as a result of the labor. Walt had never stopped blaming himself for Miranda's death. Unwittingly, he'd blamed Jesse as well, and had spent the next several years trying to ignore his mistake. Jesse had spent the same time making damn sure his father couldn't ignore him. Where Lucy had always striven to please, Jesse had shot for the opposite effect, with a vengeance. He'd always been uncannily accurate at hitting his mark.

"Walt may not have given a damn about me," he said now, "but he loved this ranch. And he knew he was insuring his legacy and the future of the Flying K when he penciled you into the picture. The way I've got it figured, he knew Lucy would want to sell out before she'd ever consider ranching again. She's seen too many hard winters, and it's a lonely life for a woman alone. And I'm sure he figured I wouldn't give a damn either way."

He offered Amanda a sip of his whiskey. When she shook her head, he continued. "You're his insurance policy, Sunshine. He knew how much you love the Flying K. I think he took a calculated risk that you would dig your heels in and refuse to sell."

Amanda confirmed his conclusions with a thoughtful silence, then said wonderingly, "Who'd have ever thought Montana ranch land would bring such a premium price."

Jesse shrugged. "I don't think it's topped out yet. In a few more months the land values here will pass those in the Bitterroot, Big Timber area. There are so many celebrities scrambling for their own little piece of paradise—which just happens to provide a tidy little tax shelter—that the sellable land is fast running out. The paper last week referred to the land boom as the 'Aspenization of Montana.'" He paused and looked directly at her. "You could save yourself a lot of backbreaking work and heartache,and pocket a sizable profit if you jumped on the wagon."

"And you and Lucy would make an even bigger haul, wouldn't you?"

Jesse smiled. "Walt put you in a hell of a spot, didn't he, Sunshine? Splitting the deeded land primarily between Lucy and me, then leaving you a strip down the middle and control of the leased acres was a stroke of genius. I'll give him credit. He was nothing if not shrewd."

"Like you said, he was protecting his legacy." That thought suddenly left Amanda feeling tired and very alone.

"And who's protecting you, Amanda?" Jesse asked softly. "The old man put you at risk, like it or not."

"I'll never agree to sell, Jess. I'm sorry if you were counting on the money from the sale—"

His laugh cut her off. "Oh, right. Willie filled me in on your assessment of my life to date. Let's see if I've got the scenario right. I'm a shiftless playboy without a dime in my pocket and undoubtedly need the money to keep me rolling in the clover to which I've become accustomed. Does that about sum it up?"

She refused to be intimidated by his mocking. Her

life, her livelihood, was at stake, and she was entitled to some answers. "Since you brought it up, do you need the money?"

"I get by," he said with a throwaway grin.

"I understand Porsches are expensive to keep up."

He shook his head chastisingly. "I thought you were through pussyfooting. Why don't you just come right out and ask me?"

"Okay. What do you do for a living?"

"Besides live off women, you mean?"

"Yes," she said, ignoring his goading smirk. "Besides that."

He considered her for a moment, then shrugged as if to say what the hell. "I've managed to sell a song or two when I needed a buck."

She glanced at the guitar resting by his chair and thought of the calluses on his fingers. "You write songs?"

"That's the long and the short of it. Sorry if that disappoints you, but it's what I do."

"And you're making money at it?"

"Don't sound so skeptical, darlin'. I do get by."

She considered him for a long moment before he broke the silence with an abrupt change of subject. "Did you know that my father was in love with your mother?"

His question caught her off guard. She was still trying to digest the news of his career, if you could call writing songs "when I needed a buck" a career. He looked entirely too pleased with the fact that he'd thrown her, she decided, and changed her mind about the drink. Lifting the glass from his hand, she took a deep swallow.

The cool burn of iced whiskey eased the tightness in her throat and soothed the turmoil in her stomach. If Jesse expected her to act shocked at his question, he was going to be disappointed. "Yes," she answered, "I guess I always suspected. But I also know Walt loved both my mom and my dad too much to interfere with their marriage."

Jesse conceded that point with a thoughtful nod. "How are your folks anyway."

"Fine. Dad doesn't get around as well as he'd like to because of his hip, but the dry Arizona climate has been good for him. Mom's happy there too."

"I think they might have been another reason Walt included you in his will."

"How so?" she asked, wondering at the warmth that had softened his features.

"Maybe it was his way of thanking your father for being so loyal and your mother for practically raising me. I must have been a hell of a handful."

Amanda smiled at the picture that statement conjured. "You're still a handful," she said, drifting into an easy intimacy fostered by memories of Jesse as a boy, as her protector, as the one who'd held her when she cried over a skinned knee or lost toy.

Without a thought to her actions, she raised her hand to the lock of hair tumbling over his brow. She brushed it back, watching the slow, caressing sweep of her fingers.

His hair was thick and lush, as wild and unruly as a rogue stallion's untamable mane. Perpetually tousled, more than a little too long, the softly curling mass of jet-black silk appeared, always, like he'd just roused himself from a soft, warm bed. A woman's bed that smelled of man and musk and lovemaking deep in the night.

Unbidden, her gaze strayed to the utterly sensual curve of his upper lip.

Jesse's harsh, slow whisper broke the silence. "And you're as much of a temptation now as you were back then, Sunshine."

The mood shifted abruptly. The night became very

still. Amanda was overwhelmingly aware of him holding her, of the intimacy of shared body heat, of the scant barrier of silk and denim between them.

She dragged her gaze to his—and regretted it. Struggling not to respond to the suggestion shimmering in his eyes, she pulled her hand away and forced a detached smile. "And you're still as much of a bull-slinger."

He wasn't buying it. His gaze burned into hers, his invitation sultry and not at all sweet. She shivered as a lush river of anticipation gushed from her breast to the part of her that wouldn't let her forget she was a woman and Jesse was an unforgettable man.

She should be fighting this. She couldn't. She closed her eyes and stopped breathing when his hand caressed her cheek, then slid in an agonizingly slow glide down the length of her throat. His fingers spread wide across her skin and lingered before wandering to the opening of her robe.

"Silk on silk," he murmured, watching his hand explore. "Amanda, I want you."

With a jerky motion, she came to her senses. She grasped his wrist and stilled his hand. "Why do you do that?" she asked breathlessly. Desperately. "Why do you tease me so?"

He studied her. "What makes you think I'm teasing?"

"Because I know who you are, Jess. I know *what* you are. You're a rounder and a renegade. The last thing you'd want is a woman like me."

"A woman like you? And what kind of a woman is that, Amanda? Tell me, but leave out what I already know." His gaze dropped again to her breasts. "That you're a woman who wears sexy silk kimonos with nothing underneath. That you're a woman who comes midnight-calling in her bare feet. That you're a woman who responds to me."

"Stop it!" she demanded, dragging his hand away from the opening in her robe. "It's a joke for you, isn't it? I'm the furthest thing from the women you're used to. I'm your basic plain-Jane, salt of the earth, no-nonsense Girl Scout type. I wasn't what you wanted ten years ago, and I'm not what you want now. I don't understand why you're even bothering to play your games with me."

His entire body suddenly became still. She took advantage of his pensiveness to show him the extent of her anger. "Do you get some twisted kick out of raising the little tomboy's blood pressure? Will it be a real hoot to go back to your ladies and tell them about me?"

"What I'd like to know," he said in a tone as angry as her own, "is who the hell's been feeding you all the crap about me? And where, on God's green earth, are they getting their information?"

Amanda was puzzled at the denial in his voice and expression. If she didn't know better, she would think she'd hit a sore spot. But it was safer fighting with him than wondering if the stories were true. So she persisted. "Your exploits are legend around here."

"In whose songbook?" he roared like he'd been wounded.

"Everybody's!" she fired back, and tried to stand up.

He jerked her back down. "Everybody's? As in your father's?"

"My father has nothing to do with this."

He uttered a low growl. "Your father, Little Mary Sunshine, has *everything* to do with this. Granted, he's a good man, but he always had a hell of a case against me. He's the one who painted all those pretty pictures of me. He's the one who warned you from the time you were trying to fill out your training bra that I was bad news."

Amanda reared back with every intention of knocking him into next week. Jesse saw it coming. He snagged her arm, twisted it behind her back, and hauled her up against him. Ignoring her gasp of surprise, he manacled her wrist with one hand and fisted the other around a handful of her hair.

Holding her so their mouths were all but touching, he forced her to look at him. "You think I didn't ache for you all those times you turned your liquid brown eyes on me? Eyes that said, I want you? You think it wasn't one of the most noble acts this outlaw ever committed when I resisted the sweet temptation of introducing you to your first taste of passion? You hated me then for not taking what I knew you wanted to give. I hated myself for not taking it."

His control was ultimate and total as he whispered, "Don't hate me now, Amanda, not for doing the right thing all those years ago. Just give. Give what we've both waited ten long years for me to take."

Three

Without a thought of denial, without an ounce of repentance, Jesse lowered his mouth and took hers. He kissed her hard, kissed her long. Openmouthed, wet, and hungry, he poured into the kiss all the anger that threatened to overtake him, all the passion that promised to undo him. When at last she surrendered and stirred, threading her free hand into his hair and pulling him closer, he kissed her with all the tenderness her sweet, yielding mouth deserved.

"Amanda," he whispered brokenly, unstrung from the inside out by her sudden and total response. "Sweet, sweet Amanda." He untangled his hand from her hair and went in search of her breast.

Her arms wound possessively around his neck. She arched her back to give him access to the supple flesh beneath her robe. Murmuring her pleasure, she pressed herself into his kneading hand.

Lost in the heat of her mouth, the silk of her skin, the awakening of her as a woman, Jesse didn't notice when she tensed and began to struggle.

"Jess . . . Jess, stop," she pleaded, finally managing to twist her head away. "Please. This can't happen."

"Too late," he murmured, dragging her back against him. "It's happening."

With a frustrated groan, she gripped handfuls of his hair and pulled.

"Ouch, dammit!"

She took advantage of his anger to put a few inches of moonlight between them. "I don't want this, Jess," she whispered breathlessly. "I don't need this in my life right now."

He rubbed his burning scalp ruefully. "A simple no would have done nicely. You didn't have to scalp me."

"A simple no has never worked where you're concerned."

He looked at her long and hard. "That's because there's nothing simple about our relationship."

"We don't have a relationship, Jesse. Please . . . let's keep it that way."

He shook his head, hearing the denial of her words yet seeing the truth in her eyes. "You want me."

She swallowed hard and looked away. "I want you to leave me alone."

Before he could respond, a light came on in the dark ranch house behind him. Its pale glow spilled outside, illuminating the patio tile and casting dark shadows on Amanda's face as she looked over his shoulder.

Jesse didn't have to turn around to know what Amanda saw. Her stricken expression painted a vivid picture. Carolyn had awakened and come looking for him.

He swore under his breath.

"Jesse?" Carolyn's sultry voice, full of Southern heat, echoed in the darkness, shattering the edgy silence like crystal struck by stone.

"Jesse, are you out there?" Carolyn called hesitantly.

Gripping Amanda's shoulders, Jesse forced her to look at him. "Amanda—"

"Your *errand*, I take it?" Her stone-cold stare dared him to try to explain.

"Honey, it's not what you think."

Amanda pulled away from him. She looked at the blonde woman in the black negligee, then back at the man who'd riddled her pride.

"Nothing ever is," she said numbly.

Without another word, she eased off his lap and walked away.

Without a word in his defense, Jesse let her go.

First light had yet to make an appearance, when a distant ringing blasted the silence in Amanda's bedroom like a flashlight slicing into darkness. Not that the shrill sound woke her. What little sleep she had managed to steal since midnight wasn't worth logging in hours.

Exhausted, she stumbled into the kitchen to answer the phone. "Yes, hello," she said softly, shoving a handful of hair away from her heavy-lidded eyes.

She listened for a minute, then finally interrupted the distraught rambling on the other end of the line. "Tina . . . Tina, it's all right. You can't help it. I understand . . . No, no, don't worry about it. I'm sure I can handle it. How tough can it be, right?" She forced a false brightness into her voice. "You take care of your daughter and enjoy that new baby. I'll see you, well, when I see you. And, Tina, congratulations, Gramma." Amanda laughed softly. "I'm sure you'll get used to it. Now, don't worry. We'll get along fine for a few days. . . . Uh-huh. You too. 'Bye."

Slumping down on the cold oak chair beside the

phone, Amanda dangled limp hands between her bare legs.

"Well." She sighed in begrudging acceptance and muttered what she already knew too well to be true. "Nobody ever said it would be easy."

Shouting distance was as close as Amanda wanted to get to Jesse Kincannon after the previous night. Yet at five A.M., dressed in her boots and blue jeans and a warm flannel shirt to ward off the chill of the late spring morning, she slipped inside the kitchen to take over Tina's cooking duties.

The big house was dark and silent. It matched her mood. Matched her thoughts of the man asleep down the hall. And of the woman, whoever she was, curled up in bed beside him.

"Pity her, Amanda," she mumbled, trying to banish the picture that thought conjured as she hurriedly mixed biscuit dough for the dozen hungry ranch hands who would converge on the kitchen within the hour. "Just be glad it isn't you. Be glad you came to your senses before he . . ." Gripping the edge of the kitchen counter with flour-coated fingers, she pinched back tears of humiliation. That was the worst part. She *hadn't* come to her senses. In fact, she'd lost sight of all reason.

The night before she'd been close to following Jesse Kincannon anywhere he'd wanted to take her. Anywhere. She'd been lost in his hungry kisses, drowning in his silken caress. Painful as it was to admit, if that woman hadn't made her dramatic appearance when she had, Amanda would have been one more conquest for Jesse Kincannon to boast about.

She hated him for what he'd done to her.

She hated herself more.

"Where's Tina?"

Amanda spun around, startled by Jesse's sleep-graveled voice behind her. Caught unprepared, she simply stared.

He'd slipped on his jeans—barely—and nothing else. The top two brass snaps lay open. The dark hair beneath the placket arrowed aggressively toward the masculine contours hidden within. Fresh from his bed, his hair as rumpled and tousled as she suspected his sheets were, he gripped the door frame above his head. With his weight slung onto one long, cowboy-lean leg, he stretched out the morning stiffness. But it was the look in his eyes that launched the most vicious assault on her jagged senses. And she remembered too vividly the touch of his mouth on hers.

She would never let him get to her that way again, she vowed. Nor would she ever let him know how much he'd hurt her. Turning back to the stove, she slid the sheet of biscuits into the oven and started working on the sausage gravy.

"Tina had to go to Billings," she said. "Her daughter delivered her baby early last night." The steadiness of her voice surprised her. It no way matched the beat of her heart. "Mom and baby girl are fine, but Tina's going to stay with them for a few days."

"So Tina's a gramma," Jesse said with a smile in his voice.

Amanda nodded and put the sausage on to fry. Even with her back to him, Jesse's image was imprinted in her mind. No man had a right to look as appealing as the one filling up the kitchen doorway.

His pose couldn't have been more taunting if he'd planned it, yet somehow, she knew he hadn't. He didn't have to. Everything Jesse did, every move he made, was totally sensual. Even the fine sprinkling of hair under his arms was sexy. And his voice, when he spoke again, was as morning-rough as the stubble of dark beard shadowing his face, as whiskey-mellow as a sultry, beckoning dream.

"Is there coffee?"

Without turning away from the stove, she gestured toward the percolator on the counter. "Help yourself."

She heard him cross the kitchen and open a cupboard door.

"Can I pour you a cup?"

"Sure," she answered brightly. Too brightly.

He settled in close. Too close.

From the corner of her eye, she watched his dark nipples pucker tight against the morning chill. Making a monumental effort to avoid looking at the lean hips propped against the counter beside her, she raised the mug to her lips . . . and promptly burned her tongue.

"Damn!" she sputtered, slamming the mug down on the counter.

"You okay?" he asked, solicitously patting her on the back.

"I'm fine!" she snapped, and ran the back of her hand across her burning mouth. She whirled on him, shrugging away his touch. "I'd be a hell of a lot better if you'd just find someplace else to park your"—her gaze roamed frantically from one gloriously muscled expanse of naked skin to another—"self," she finished lamely. Spinning away from him, she attacked the pan of sausage sizzling on the stove. "Can't you find somewhere to light other than in this kitchen?"

"Bothers you, does it, Amanda?"

She didn't have to face him to know he was grinning. The smugness in his voice told her as much. "You're in my way. That's all."

"Maybe I could give you a hand with—"

She cut him off with a sharp look and a proud tilt of her chin. "I don't need any help." She had to bite her tongue to keep from adding "from the likes of you."

Evidently, she'd as good as said it. His stance changed from playful goading to serious threat in one smooth motion.

He stalked toward her. She held her ground . . . until he smiled. Her pride was still too bruised to provide defense against his ridicule, and she'd been too recently fooled to believe the kindness in his eyes. She backed up quickly. It was a major tactical error.

The next thing she knew, she had the stove at her back and over six feet of determined Kincannon pressed against her front. She couldn't say which obstacle generated the most heat.

"Read my lips, Kincannon," she said succinctly. "You're in my way."

"Get used to it, Carter," he answered, mimicking her clipped delivery. His voice was as cool as frost on a freezer door. But his breath, as it fluttered against her cheek, was as hot as the skillet behind her. "Because like it or not, you're going to find me in your way until you're ready to listen to me about Carolyn."

Carolyn. Somehow, the sting was sharper now that the unknown woman had a name. Carolyn. It fit the slender blonde in the black negligee. Had she had a good laugh with Jesse last night?

"Amanda, look at me."

She did, her eyes bright and shining, her chin lifted high. Jesse almost laughed. He would have if he hadn't been concerned for his own health. "Not like you want to roll me in flour and stuff me in the oven with your biscuits."

"It bears thinking about," she returned dryly, and lowered her gaze once more.

"Carolyn is a friend. Nothing more. She needs a place to do some thinking and to rest. She's going through a rough time right now. You need to trust me on this, Sunshine."

Fighting for a shred of composure, Amanda forced herself to meet his gaze again. Another monumental blunder. Those damn devil eyes of his.

"Look," she began, somehow managing to sound unaffected, "what you do and who you do it to is your affair, not mine. I don't want to hear about your women. And I don't want to be included in your games."

Jesse looked at her long and hard, then skimmed his knuckles along the determined set of her jaw. His hand descended to the base of her throat, where Amanda knew her pulse fluttered wildly. "He must have been a real jerk," he said finally as his gaze slid back up to hers.

She swallowed against the light pressure of his hand. "What are you talking about?"

"Not what, Amanda." Jesse's voice was as silky as the stroke of his thumb against her throat. "Who. I'm referring to the man who hurt you. He must have been a real bastard to strip your confidence this way."

Stung by his insight, she shoved his hand away. "Pot calling the kettle black, Jess?" she lashed out.

His eyes hardened, but his gaze never left her face.

She met it boldly. "You had your fun. Now, stay out of my way. I've got work to do. I'm sure you do too. Surely you've got some more *errands* to run . . . or to run after."

Shouldering past him, she pushed through the pantry door in search of something, anything, that would get her out of striking distance of his eyes.

"You know, Sunshine," he drawled from the kitchen, seemingly unperturbed as he rattled around, helping himself to more coffee. "That temper of yours is going to get you in a whole lot of hot wat—"

"Jesse!" Willie slammed through the kitchen door,

cutting Jesse off midsentence. "Thank God you're up! We got trouble, boy."

Amanda stepped quickly out of the pantry. There was a look of stark terror in the old foreman's eyes.

"Willie?"

Willie's wry frame slumped with relief when he saw her. "Amanda! God, girl, I was afraid you were in the barn."

"Willie, what's wrong?"

"We got us a fire, honey," he said gently. His hands shook as he worried his battered Stetson between them. "It's the barn." He swore under his breath as Amanda's eyes grew wide with terror, then quickly added, "Now, don't you worry. The boys are already workin' on it."

Momentarily stunned, Amanda walked on rubbery legs toward the door, tugging frantically at the towel she'd knotted around her waist as an apron. She grabbed her jacket from the peg on the wall and struggled into it. "Jesse, call the county fire department. The number's by the phone."

"Hold it." Jesse snagged her wrist, stopping her from heading out the door. "You make the call, Amanda, then keep clear of that barn until we get this thing under control. Do you understand me?"

He gave her a hard look when she resisted. "We're wasting time. Make that call!"

Without a backward glance, he loped up the stairs to grab his boots and a shirt, shouting more orders on the way. "Willie, if you haven't done it already, start moving out what stock you can get to and have the boys get the machinery that's worth saving out of harm's way."

"Oh, God, Willie!" Amanda cried as the full implication of the fire sank in. "Eclipse and Topper?"

"They'll be all right, girl. We'll get your horses out. You just get us some help here, okay?"

For one brief moment before Willie sailed outside, his eyes met hers. The look in them reflected too clearly what Amanda was thinking. Any other morning she would have been in the barn right now. Anyone who worked for or was associated with the Flying K knew that at first light, she headed straight for Eclipse's stall to give the old stallion his morning rubdown.

Every morning, without fail, she'd go down to the barn alone. Every morning, but this one. Less than an hour ago, even she hadn't known that her morning plans would be changed. Whoever had started the fire hadn't known either.

By seven o'clock that night, the last threat of a flare-up was finally over. Eclipse was all right. Her little mare, Topper, was too. It was Jesse who'd gotten them out. Jesse, who'd thrown a water-soaked blanket over his shoulders and dragged the screaming stallion and terrified mare free of the smoke and flames.

Slumped on the ground with her back propped against a tractor tire, Amanda watched an orange-red sun sink behind the purple ridge of the mountains.

She was too tired to be hostile toward the woman walking toward her. She was too relieved to be anything but grateful that it was over and they hadn't lost any more than they had. But she was also too much woman not to die a little inside when she raised her soot-streaked face to the serene and beautiful Carolyn, who approached her with a mug of coffee held in her carefully manicured hand.

An even break, Amanda mused, was evidently too much to ask for.

Physically, she and Carolyn weren't that different. Amanda was merely packaged with a little less panache. Carolyn was a willowy, sophisticated blonde, her hair precision cut in a stunning, long pageboy. Amanda was a slim, unpretentious tomboy with a mop of wild yellow hair that was currently streaked with ash and smoke, and singed on the ends from her one close brush with the fire.

Carolyn extended the mug.

Amanda took it. To do otherwise would have been ungrateful. Besides, it gave her something to do with her hands . . . her filthy, scratched, and way-past-the-need-for-a-manicure hands.

She hadn't thought she had it in her, but she heard herself saying, "Thanks."

Carolyn gazed at her for an uncomfortable moment. "You look exhausted."

Exhausted was no doubt a kind word for how she looked, Amanda thought. She didn't want this Southern belle's kindness. "Yeah, well, next time someone throws me a surprise fire, I'll make sure I get a nap in beforehand."

To her surprise, the woman in the jade silk blouse and dove-gray pleated trousers smiled at her. "I know you don't want to hear this, but I wish we could have met under different circumstances."

Amanda threw her an incredulous look. "You're right. I don't want to hear this."

If she'd had the strength to get up and walk away, she would have. She didn't, though, so she had to settle for diverting her gaze to the scene before her.

The barn was no longer smoldering. The structural damage had, thank heavens, been minimal and confined to the south end. No livestock had been lost and only a small percentage of the hay they'd put up the week before had been ruined.

The biggest casualty appeared not to be fire related. The biggest casualty was another hit to Amanda's pride.

Jesse had moved in and taken over, efficiently, effectively. The men had looked instinctively to him for guidance. They'd been right to do so. For all her certainty that she could handle it, she had frozen. She'd seen the smoke billowing out the south door, heard the frantic screams of the horses still trapped inside, and she'd panicked.

Jesse hadn't. Jesse had been magnificent. Even now, as tired as he had to be, he moved with purpose and ease among the men, working alongside them as they cleaned up the last of the mess.

Amanda closed her eyes and rested her head against the hard rubber tire. Who did she think she was kidding? What had ever made her think she could run a ranch?

And niggling away in the back of her mind was the question she'd avoided asking herself all day. Was someone really trying to kill her?

Jake Slater slunk past her carrying a coiled water hose. She shivered at the hostility in his eyes until Carolyn's irritatingly silky and yet compassionate voice snapped her back to the moment. "There are sandwiches and more coffee inside. I'm sure you could do with a little—"

"I'm fine," Amanda cut her off, and was immediately ashamed of the bitterness she heard in her own voice. Carolyn's kindness was simply more than she could take right then. The woman seemed incapable of doing anything that Amanda could fault her for. Even now she seemed to sense Amanda's need for solitude. Without a word of admonishment, she turned and quietly walked away.

All day, as Amanda had avoided the fire, working instead with a team of men to adapt the old stallion barn into temporary space for the stock, she'd been aware of Carolyn's calm presence in the midst of frantic activity. Cucumber cool, she'd glided in and out of the house, offering coffee, food, a smile of encouragement for the men, and a special, intimate smile of support and pride for Jesse.

Jesse. Amanda closed her eyes and let the fatigue and the wanting take over. The fire had threatened to destroy the ranch, and damn her stupid, simpering hide, all she could think about, all she wanted, was Jesse. Jesse to hold her. Jesse to make her feel safe. Jesse to love her . . . the way her foolish, foolish heart had chosen to love him.

It was well on to ten o'clock before Jesse, alone outside for the past hour since sending the men in for supper, let the exhaustion of the day catch up with him. He was in the process of making one last check around the barn when Willie found him.

"We were lucky today," the older man said. "Coulda lost the whole damn barn and everything in it."

Jesse nodded and waited for the questions he knew would follow.

Willie asked the first one. "What did Chief Jackson have to say?"

"Not much. He'll be sending the fire marshal out in the morning to look things over."

"Any chance it coulda been an accident?" Willie asked with none of the hope in his voice that was in the question.

Jesse shrugged. "There's a chance, sure. Maybe spontaneous combustion. Could have been a hundred different things that set off that fire."

Willie nodded. "Sure. Coulda been."

Both men knew differently. Both knew the fire had been no accident.

"I don't want nothin' happening to the girl, Jesse."

The warning in Willie's statement was glaringly clear. "Nothing's going to happen to her, Willie. Not as long as I'm here. Where is she anyway? I haven't seen her since sunset."

The old cowhand met Jesse's eyes in the darkness. It was a testing look, a measuring look, that changed after a moment to a look of acceptance. He pointed in the direction of the tack house, then walked away.

Jesse found her in the shadows of the hulking tractor, slumped against a wheel sound asleep. He shoved his hands in his hip pockets and gazed down at the bedraggled, dirt-streaked bundle of woman, who at the moment looked more like a lost little child. An incredible, protective feeling of warmth seemed to flood his heart.

He hunkered down in front of her and gently rubbed her shoulder. "Hey, cowgirl, wake up," he said softly. "The roundup's over. Time for all the little buckaroos and buckarettes to head for the bunkhouse.

She opened her eyes slowly, blinked, then scowled. "Jess?"

For the first time since Willie had burst into the kitchen that morning, he felt like grinning. "Yes, darlin'. It's Jess."

"I—I fell asleep."

"More like passed out. That's what happens to people who push themselves from dawn to dusk every day. They have a tendency to wear out. Then, when something really stressful comes along . . ." He let his voice trail off when he realized she'd conked out on him again.

He shook his head, damning himself for letting it come to this. He'd pushed her to this state of exhaustion. He was responsible for the schedule she'd set for herself each day since he'd shown up. And he was responsible for the sleep he suspected she'd missed last night.

And don't forget today, Jess, he admonished himself. Oh, yes, he was responsible for that, too, no matter how reluctant he was to admit it.

"One thing at a time," he murmured aloud when she moaned and shivered in her sleep.

"All right, Amanda. Come on. It's getting cold out here. That's my girl," he crooned as he urged her to her feet with some gentle pressure on her elbow. "Let's get you up off this hard-packed dirt and into your nice soft bed. That's it. Upsy-daisy."

She mumbled something unintelligible, but Jesse thought he picked up the words, "hands off me," as she struggled to rise under her own steam.

Fighting a grin, he held her arm while she got her balance. "Can you stand up? Whoops, I didn't think so." He swept her quickly into his arms just as her knees buckled.

"Jess . . . I—I can . . . walk. Put me down."

That came out loud and clear. "Honey, you can't even stand, let alone walk. Now, hush. It's late and you're dead tired." He hefted her higher against his chest. "I'm putting you to bed."

"I don't want you anywhere near my bed, Jesse Kincannon."

He laughed. "You lie, Amanda Carter. But that's an argument for another night. Now, quit fidgeting and help me. Put your arms around my neck."

Apparently, she was too tired to sustain the struggle. She wrapped her arms around his neck like a good girl and snuggled closer. And more melting took place in Jesse's chest.

After managing to open her cottage door without dropping her, Jesse felt his way in the darkness to her bedroom. He flipped on a light with his elbow, then laid her gently on her double brass bed. He didn't give a damn if he soiled the pale yellow satin comforter with ash and the smell of smoke.

"Jesse, what are you doing?"

"Shhh." He dropped one of her dusty boots to the floor and started tugging on the other. "I'm just getting you comfortable. Now, hush. For once, be good."

That job done, he found and wet a washcloth in her bathroom. Returning to the bedroom, he sat down, his hip making light contact with hers when his weight sank into the mattress. Taking special care of her face, he wiped the grime away.

Her skin was so pale, the fragile tissue beneath her eyes a faded, bruised violet. He wanted to love her awake, ease her fatigue with arousing strokes of his hands and mouth that would please them both. He fought to ignore the tight, insistent ache in his groin. *Not tonight, Jess.* Not when she could hide behind the excuse of exhaustion tomorrow.

Setting his jaw in grim determination, he reached for the snap on her jeans. His eyebrows arched when she made no effort to fight him. He had the zipper down and a grip on the waistband before she seemed to realize what was going on.

"Jesse," she protested drowsily, covering his hands with her own. "No."

"Amanda," he scolded, his voice taking on the tone of a parent dealing with an obstinate but cherished child. "Quit your fussing. I just want to get you out of these clothes."

"I bet you want to get Carolyn out of her clothes, too, don't you?" she asked in a petulant, half-lucid pique.

"Carolyn can undress herself just fine without my help," he said, grinning. "You, Sunshine, cannot. Not at the moment anyway. Come on, now, help me. Lift your hips."

She complied, seemingly caught somewhere between consciousness and reluctant complacency.

By the time Jesse had slid her dusty jeans down over her hips and watched her legs squirm impatiently to get free of the encumbering denim, he was thinking maybe his good intentions weren't going to be enough to get him through this.

Her hips were slim. The pale flesh visible above and below her briefs was as smooth and unblemished as porcelain, as soft and enticing as a summer dream. Her legs were long and silky, as lean and fluidly muscled as a yearling's. An odd jealousy flashed through him as he thought of that old stallion she sat so tight every day. One day soon, he promised, it would be his hips she wrapped her legs around. His hips she'd cling to and hold on tight.

With increasing difficulty, he tucked away that image and steered his hands and his gaze to the buttons on her flannel shirt . . . and found himself in trouble again.

"Sit up, honey," he ordered raggedly as he wrapped a supporting arm around her back.

She was all pliant, shimmering heat when she fell forward against his chest. He quickly stripped the shirt from her and held her protectively against him. Her heavy sigh was childlike as she snuggled in complete trust against his shoulder. There was nothing childlike about her breasts pressing into his chest, though. Nor was there anything paternal about the emotion clutching him low in his gut.

"It takes a desperate man," she murmured between yawns, "to seduce a defenseless, half-conscious woman."

He chuckled at her tenacity and, with reluctance, laid her back down. "In the first place," he said, brushing her hair away from her forehead, "you have never been and will never be defenseless. And I'm neither desperate nor foolish enough to want to make love to you when you don't even know what you're doing. When the time comes, Amanda, we'll both be lucid. And we'll both be ready."

"Don't hold your breath, cowboy."

Jesse grinned. She was as punch-drunk with fatigue as a sailor who'd drunk up his shore leave, but she'd fight him to the bitter end. "Is that any way for a lady to talk?" He tugged down the hem of her undershirt until it reached the top of her jockey-style cotton briefs. "And is this any way for a lady to dress? I've never seen such ugly underwear."

"You leave my underwear out of this."

"Oh, I'd like to, sweetheart. But as I said, not tonight."

He covered her carefully with the quilt, then eased off the bed and walked quietly to the window.

He heard her stir, silken skin against antique satin.

"Jesse."

"I'm right here, Amanda. Just closing the curtains so you can sleep in tomorrow morning."

"Jess . . ."

He heard the fear in her voice, sensed the tears gathering. He'd been waiting all day for it to hit her. Thanking the Lord that he was with her when it did, he quickly returned to the bed and pulled her up against him.

"It's all right, baby."

"I—I couldn't," she whispered, desperately clutching handfuls of his shirt. "Oh, God, the fire! I couldn't go in there."

"Shhh, baby. Nobody expected you to. Nobody needed you to."

She pushed away from him, her eyes wild with fear. "Why? Why is this happening?"

Stricken by the vulnerability in her voice, he

crushed her in his arms. "I don't know, babe. I don't know."

Feeling helpless and angry, Jesse gave her the only answers he could offer. He listened while she sobbed, held her while she trembled, and rocked her until she finally fell asleep.

Four

Amanda didn't have to see a clock to know it was well past noon when she woke up the next day. The sun was high. Its light filled her bedroom, warming it, as the shade on the south window fluttered slowly up to half-mast.

Neither did she have to open her eyes to know who stood by that window waiting for her to come around. The scent of Carolyn's expensive perfume drifted through the bedroom like a haughty whisper, reminding Amanda of the other woman's involvement with Jesse. Jesse. She'd had a foolish dream that he'd stayed with her last night. That he'd watched over her.

Trying to deny the hollow ache of disappointment, she opened her eyes and focused on the woman in the rustling silk blouse. It was all she could do to suppress a groan at the sight of Carolyn's cool beauty. In contrast, Amanda knew that she looked like something a very indiscriminate cat had dragged in.

Sitting up slowly, she shoved her hands through

the tangle of limp hair that fell across her eyes. Eyes that still burned from smoke and from crying.

Carolyn turned to face her. "I was beginning to think you were going to be out for another few hours."

Amanda propped her elbows on updrawn knees and cradled her head in her hands. Wishing for the one thing she shouldn't want, she asked the question before she could stop herself. "Where's Jesse?"

"Probably asleep in the saddle, judging by the way he looked when I found him here at five this morning."

Amanda's head came up at that. She was too drained to care that her eyes revealed her surprise.

"He spent the night here," Carolyn explained as she walked to the foot of the bed. "In that rocker. He'd still be here if I hadn't insisted he go eat breakfast. Even then, the only way he'd leave was if I promised to stay until you woke up."

Amanda's heart gave a joyous leap. Joy turned instantly to puzzlement, though. Jesse had a warm, willing woman to share his bed, yet he'd stayed with her last night? She stared at Carolyn with utter bafflement. "Why?"

Carolyn crossed her arms over her breasts and returned Amanda's stare with a measuring frown. "Why did he spend the night here, or why would Jesse's 'lover' be willing to take over the vigil?"

Somehow, Amanda managed not to flinch. Silence, however, was the best response she could muster to answer Carolyn's challenging look.

"If you can't figure it out," Carolyn said finally, "I don't think I should be the one to tell you."

Amanda remained silent.

Carolyn shook her head. "You're really something, you know that? You're as stubborn as Jesse gives you credit for, but you're not near as smart."

Amanda bit back one retort, considered another one, then let it go. It was hard arguing with the truth. She *was* stubborn, and she'd proven she wasn't very smart. At least not where Jesse was concerned. She didn't know what Carolyn's game was, but she wasn't having any of it. And she wasn't willing to wait around to be the punch line for someone else's bad joke.

She shoved back the covers and swung her feet to the floor. "I'm sure it'd be just buckets of fun to stay here and trade insults with you," she said, affecting her best Scarlett O'Hara drawl. "But I've got work to do. You can tell Jesse you fulfilled your duty. I'm sure he'll be pleased as punch and come up with some deliciously expressive way to reward you for your . . ." she paused, subjected Carolyn to a blatantly insulting look, and finished, "diligence."

Pushing herself off the bed, she strode toward the bathroom. "If you'll excuse me, I need a shower."

Amanda shut the door carefully behind her, determined not to lose control. Leaning back against the door, she closed her eyes and told herself she could handle this. But the stench of the fire and the memory of the previous day's fear clung like a bad dream and mingled with a picture of Jesse "rewarding" Carolyn.

She stripped off her underwear, driven by a sudden and nearly violent urge to wash away every one of those images. Twisting the faucets on full blast, she raised her face to the stinging spray.

Though Amanda could usually count on a hot shower to make her feel better, this one didn't. She was calmer, though. When she finally emerged from the bathroom wrapped in her kimono, she halfway hoped to find Carolyn waiting so she could apologize.

She was ashamed of her bitchy behavior. It wasn't like her to be hateful and mean, and she wasn't comfortable with herself because of it. Besides, it was none of her business what went on between Carolyn and Jesse. *Jesse* wasn't her business; the ranch was. And from the way things were going, she'd best concentrate on that.

But Carolyn wasn't there when Amanda slipped back into her bedroom. Jesse was. The wild thundering of her heart thoroughly trampled what little calm she'd managed to get a grip on.

The towel she'd been dragging through her hair went limp in her hands as she took in the sight and the scent and the statement Jesse made lying across her old brass bed.

He was sound asleep, stretched out in all his long-limbed glory, his dusty Stetson tugged over his eyes. With his booted feet crossed at the ankles, his arms pillowing his dark head, he looked for all the world like he owned that bed and, by implication, the woman who spent her nights in it.

The anger Amanda wanted to feel wouldn't come. A rush of tenderness shouldered it out of the way. Jesse was exhausted because of her. Because he'd stayed up all night watching over her.

Just when she had him figured for a user, he pulled something like this. She wanted to believe he cared, that he was human and kind, capable of feelings for someone other than himself. "Damn you, Jesse Kincannon," she swore under her breath as she crept toward the enigmatic man on her bed.

He was covered from head to toe in faded denim, pale blue chambray, and a light film of trail dust. He looked positively beautiful and unaccountably vulnerable, though Amanda suspected that if anyone was vulnerable at this moment, it was she.

Even though his hat covered the eyes that teased,

the hair that begged to be ruffled, she could see his features clearly in her mind—just as she knew she would see them for the rest of her life. He smelled of man and musk and saddle leather, a combination that stirred in her the desire to be the woman she knew he could make her become.

His long, lean frame invited her to join him on the bed. And Lord help her, she wanted to, though she stopped herself just short of reaching out and touching him. She wanted him to fold her in his arms and tell her she didn't have to be afraid again. That he'd always be there for her. That he loved her and needed her and that women like Carolyn didn't exist in his life.

Shaking her head in disgust, Amanda reminded herself that she had once wanted to believe in fairy tales, too, but she'd given up on "happily ever after" when she'd found Todd Hamilton in her best friend's bed.

Swallowing back the pain that always accompanied Todd's memory, she dragged the towel through her hair. If she had a lick of sense, she'd scream at Jesse to get the hell off her bed and out of her house. But she didn't have any sense. Not where he was concerned. Hadn't she proven that already?

All she had to do was look at him, and common sense slipped away like snow off the Rockies when the Chinooks swept over them in the spring. From the tip of his scarred boots, to his sleek, muscled thighs, the tight, lean hips, and the fullness of his masculinity straining against his jeans, he intrigued her. What would it be like, she wondered, to be loved by Jesse Kincannon?

Her gaze crept lingeringly across his body and finally climbed to his face. Her heart jumped to her throat when she discovered he'd pushed back his Stetson and lay watching her. His lazy smile and dancing eyes told her he'd been awake for some time, that he'd seen the hungry way she'd stared at him. Pride, and only pride, kept her from turning away from his knowing look.

"I'd say we're making some definite progress here, Sunshine," he said as he took his own sweet time studying her, his hot gaze sweeping from her head to her toes, snagging briefly on the hem of her short kimono. "No need to just look, you know. You can touch. Anytime. Anywhere. Any way you want to."

His blatant invitation and unrepentant arrogance put everything back into perspective. "Don't flatter yourself, Kincannon," she said smoothly, refusing to let him know he'd rattled her. "I was just surprised to find you here, that's all."

"Come on, Amanda. Did you really think I'd leave you alone after last night?"

His voice had dropped even lower, his tone suggesting her conclusions had hurt him. His eyes hinted the same. She steeled herself against believing it. "I can take care of myself, Jess. And I'd say your halo is a little too tarnished for you to play the part of the guardian angel with any real conviction."

Expelling a tired sigh, Jesse tossed his hat onto the chair by the bed and propped himself higher on her pillows. He dragged his hands across his face, then riffled them through his hair before gracing her with an infuriatingly cocky grin.

"You're right, of course. Opportunist that I am, I only stayed the night because I didn't want to miss the big moment if you woke up willing."

She shook her head in annoyance. "Why do you always do that?"

He laced his hands behind his head and got comfortable. "Do what?"

"Make a joke of everything."

"Sweetheart," he said, his expression sober and,

she thought, even sad, "if you can't accept that the reason I stayed last night is because I care about you, then it *was* a joke."

Uncomfortable with his assessment, she turned away. She crossed the room to her dresser and picked up her hairbrush. Aware of his intense gaze on her, she ran her thumb across the bristles and listened to the bed springs creak as he shifted his weight. For a suspended moment she was bombarded with thoughts of the sounds they could make on that bed together. Struggling to free herself of the erotic image, she dragged the brush through her wet hair.

"You didn't need to stay," she said tightly. "I'm sorry I put you out."

"If you're trying to thank me," he said in a quiet voice, "why don't you just come right out and say it, instead of questioning why I did it? Can't you trust me, Amanda? Just a little? Do you always have to look for an ulterior motive?"

She faced him then, her chin held high, her eyes bright with fire. "You're the one who taught me all about ulterior motives, Jess. Maybe you taught me too well."

He closed his eyes briefly, then watched as she turned back to her dressing table and resumed her attack on her hair.

"The lessons we learn at sixteen should color our future, not rule it," he said finally. "People change, Amanda. It's called growing up. Most people forgive the sins of a child as just that . . . the sins of a child."

Amanda lowered the brush slowly, feeling herself weakening because of the truth in his words.

"Are you going to make me pay forever," he asked, "for one day a lifetime ago when I had a little too much sap flowing and 'copped a feel' behind the barn?"

She laughed sharply. "Not only are you crude, you're nowhere near the mark." Too late, she realized her mistake. Her careless remark was the same as an admission that he was capable of hurting her. Why could he always get to her this way? She fussed absently with the lid on her dusting powder, then raised her eyes to the dressing table mirror. Jesse's gaze locked on hers in the glass.

"Or are you still angry," he went on in a softer voice, "because I stopped with just that one touch when you wanted so much more? Those few steamy kisses have haunted me for years. What do you say, Sunshine? There's nothing to stop me now, no sense of honor keeping me from stealing your schoolgirl innocence."

She boldly held his gaze. "Where do you get off talking about honor?" Without speaking her name, she'd changed the subject to Carolyn.

"You're wrong, you know. You're wrong about my relationship with Carolyn."

"What you refuse to accept," she said stiffly, fighting the hypnotic pull of his eyes, "is that I don't give a damn about your relationship with Carolyn. The only thing I want from you is to leave so I can get dressed and go see to dinner for the men."

"Carolyn's taking care of the men."

Amanda snorted as she touched the powder puff to her throat. "I'll just bet she is."

With a vivid oath, Jesse reared up and snagged her arm. He yanked her onto her back on the bed before she even had time to react. Pinning her arms above her head, he leaned over her, meeting her nose-to-nose. "I've had about as much of this spoiled brat act as I can handle, Sunshine. You've been through a rough twenty-four hours, I'll give you that. But you damn well ought to be thanking Carolyn, not bad-mouthing her. She's done nothing but help you and you've let your petty jealousy—"

"Jealousy?" she shrieked, struggling against the grip of his hands.

"Yes, jealousy!" He threw his thigh across hers, stilling her thrashing legs. "And the sooner you admit it, the sooner we can deal with these feelings we have for each other and—"

"I don't have any feelings for you other than contempt," she spat.

"Fine!" he roared back, his breath as hot as his body pressing her into the bed. "Let's talk about that then."

"Look, Kincannon, just because you own half of this ranch doesn't give you the right to come waltzing in here anytime you want. I resent the hell out of it!" Despite the raw anger she sensed he was fighting to contain, she met his glare straight on. "And I resent the fact that you took over yesterday, then put me to bed like a little child who can't take care of herself let alone run a business!"

Jesse's expression gentled as his gaze roamed across her face, taking in her overbright eyes, her flaming cheeks. Her fresh just-from-the-shower scent rose to tantalize him, and he let go of his anger.

"At last, some honesty," he said, loosening his hold on her wrists. "If I didn't know you'd blow up like a green filly under a new saddle, I'd kiss you silly as a reward." A pleased grin curved one corner of his mouth when he felt her entire body tense beneath him. "I might just do it anyway."

"You are the most arrogant, most conceited—"

"Shhh. All that sweet talk gets me hot." Grasping both of her wrists in one strong hand, he caressed her jaw with the other. "Not to mention the fact that you smell fantastic." He lowered his mouth to her neck and nuzzled. "And you feel even better. Do you have any idea what I went through last night, sitting in that chair, seeing you in this bed?"

His hot breath against her throat dissolved Amanda's shield of anger. "We were talking about the ranch," she protested feebly. "And I—I didn't invite you to my room."

"Didn't you?" he asked, ignoring her attempt to distract him by trailing a string of nibbling kisses down her neck. "Didn't you invite me with your eyes every time you thought I wasn't watching? I saw, Amanda. Those beautiful black eyes of yours speak the truth even if you won't admit it. They go all smoky and liquid when you look at me. Gives me all kinds of ideas about what else is happening inside you that I can't see."

She was sinking fast. Sensation, imagination, wanting clouded her mind. "You're a handsome man, Jess. Any woman would be drawn to you physically."

"You're not just any woman." His voice, a slow, intimate drawl, touched her as none of his tactile caresses had. "And this isn't just physical. You know that."

Much as she wanted to believe him, everything she knew about him and men like him told her he lied. "No, Jess. I don't know it. You're out for a good time, but it won't be with me. I don't want to be one more feather in your fancy cap."

The hand at her jaw tightened, forcing her to look at him. He searched her eyes for a long, intense moment, then asked, "What if I told you you're the only feather?"

The notion took root deep inside her. She savored it, clinging tightly to it, before good sense returned hauling the truth along with it. "I—I'd say you're an accomplished flirt who knows how to get what he wants. But not from me, Jess. I'm not going to compromise my principles for an easy smile from a pretty face and the promise of a quick roll in the hay."

That made him laugh, a low, seductive chuckle. "I

can see I've got my work cut out for me. But I'm a determined man, Amanda. I intend to make a believer of you." He nipped her lightly on her chin. A shock of pure electric heat sizzled from her breast to her belly.

"But until that happens," he added, "there's one little misconception I can clear up right now."

"Wh-what misconception?" she asked breathlessly.

"A roll in the hay with you, Sunshine, would never be quick. It would be long and sweet and decidedly lusty."

Amanda sucked in her breath, closing her eyes against an explosive rush of sexual awareness as his hand slid slowly to the top of her breast and lingered.

She couldn't suppress a groan. "Please . . ."

Jesse raised his head, his eyes smoldering. "Please what, Sunshine? Please stop? Please continue? Please do this?" Watching her face, he cupped her breast through the thin silk.

Her eyes slammed open.

"Or this?"

She bit her lower lip to keep from crying out as he parted her robe, revealing one full, creamy breast, one pink, tight nipple.

With the pad of his thumb, he touched her. A wanting so pure, so penetrating, stole whatever denial she'd meant to utter. He teased her with whispery strokes that incited and inflamed and caused her breath to catch in her chest, her heart to dance against the flat of his palm.

"You are so pretty," he whispered raggedly, then punctuated his accolade with a featherlight brush of his lips across her breast. "And there are so many things we could do in this bed besides argue."

With infinite tenderness, he touched the tip of his wet, wicked tongue to the crest of her straining nipple.

This time her cry escaped. She arched to him, begging silently for more, aching for something . . . something.

"You like that, don't you?"

She swallowed thickly and managed to shake her head in denial.

He chuckled deep in his throat as his open mouth brushed back and forth against her flesh, savoring, suckling.

"Then you probably won't like this either." His hand slipped to the tie at her waist. He toyed with the silk belt, testing the loose knot before raising his head. Holding her passion-fired gaze with his own, he tugged until it gave.

Amanda shivered in anticipation as he pushed the robe aside. The cool air that rushed against her naked skin was quickly replaced by his warm, rough hand.

"Tell me what else you don't like," he whispered, his eyes hazy with arousal as his long, lean fingers splayed possessively across her belly. The heel of his hand pressed in a knowing, kneading rhythm against dark blonde feminine curls. "Tell me you don't want me, Amanda. Tell me you're not wet with wanting me and I'll stop right here."

She felt his weight press her deeper into the tangled bedding while her spirit soared higher. *Yes*, she thought, desperately. *Yes, yes, I want him!* It would be so easy to let him take control, to forget that tomorrow she'd be sorry and sick with self-loathing. And ashamed that he so easily shattered her control.

A tear trickled from the corner of her eye and got lost in the hair at her temple.

Seeing it, Jesse went deadly still. He drew a deep, shaky breath, then closed her robe. After kissing her where the tear tracked down her temple, he sighed with reluctance and pulled away.

Trembling with a devastating mixture of need and relief and a betraying ache of disappointment, Amanda gazed up at him, a hundred questions in her eyes.

"If you're done distracting me," he said, smiling like a choirboy, "we can get back to the business at hand."

Her eyes widened, desire snatched away by immediate rage. "Distracting!"

Ignoring her graphic curse, Jesse sat up and drew her with him. Keeping a light hold on her hands, he shifted on the bed so they sat facing each other. "I can't do anything about the fact that we're co-owners of the ranch," he began as if the last few minutes had never happened.

Dazed, Amanda could only sit and listen.

"Walt took care of that," he continued. "So like it or not, you'll have to put up with me being here. But I *have* given you room, Amanda. You have to admit that."

When she looked away, he cupped her jaw in his hand and made her face him. "Yesterday was a different story. I *did* take over, but you'll get no apology for that. I'd do it again in a heartbeat if I thought I could keep you from getting hurt. And if you think for one minute that I would have left you alone last night to deal with what you were feeling, then you really don't know me at all. I meant to help."

She lowered her eyes, ashamed. In spite of the anger she was feeling toward him now—at least she wanted it to be anger—she remembered the comfort of his arms around her, the gentle way he'd held her until she'd fallen asleep. "You did help," she admitted brokenly. "It—it's just that . . ." Her voice trailed off with her reluctance to admit her inadequacies.

Jesse had no such compunctions. "That what? That you were scared? Hell, so was I."

Guilt tore at her. "But you didn't let it get in the way of what needed to be done. I'm responsible for this ranch and I panicked. If you hadn't been here—"

He cut her off, gently pressing his thumb to her lips. "If I hadn't been here, you would have done what you had to do."

Tears of frustration stung her eyes. "I've never felt so helpless."

"Never that, baby." He ran his knuckles in a slow caress along her jaw. "A little stunned, maybe, but you recovered like a trooper."

"I leaned on you, Jess," she said, plucking at the mussed bedclothes. "I can't do that again."

"And why not?"

His tone was so open, so full of invitation, she had to get away before she threw herself back into his arms. She rose quickly and walked to the window, parting the curtain with a trembling hand. "Because you won't always be here to lean on," she said, wanting him to deny it, yet knowing she wouldn't believe him if he did. "I appreciate the fact that you've let me run things my way. Whether you're conscious of it or not, I needed that from you. Yesterday, I saw how easy it was to stand back and let you take over."

Turning to face him, she leaned wearily against the windowsill and hugged her arms around her waist. "Consider this fair warning, Jess. I mean to run this ranch the way Walt intended, whether you like the way I'm handling things or not."

"I never said you weren't handling things, Amanda."

"Then why are you here?"

He dropped his head down, then looked at her with studied calm. "So we're back to that again, are we? Honey, I told you. I'm not interested in the Flying K. What I'm interested in is you."

He rose slowly, his gaze locked on hers. With a

prowling, purposeful stride, he walked toward her. "If what just happened on that bed didn't prove anything else, it should have proven that I care about you."

"Jesse . . ." She drew in a shaky breath as he stopped in front of her, the toes of his dusty boots wedged on either side of her bare feet. He was so close, she could see his pulse thundering beneath the tanned skin of his throat. The sensations he'd awakened when he'd pinned her beneath him on the bed surged forward in living, breathing color. The scent of his skin, the vibrancy of his hard male heat, the sensual tilt of his lips, the liquid strokes of his tongue . . . If he touched her again, she'd be a goner.

"Jess . . ." she whispered. "Please. Don't."

After what seemed like an eternity, his ragged sigh stirred the hair at her temple. "Fine," he said gruffly, and backed away. "But we're not finished with this. Not by a long shot."

Her heart beating wildly, she watched him scoop up his hat, settle it on his head, and stride across the room. "I'll wait outside the door while you get dressed and pack a bag."

She stared at his departing back, his words taking a moment to register. "Pack a bag?"

He stopped with his hand on the door. "I've decided you're going to move into the ranch house . . . at least until this mess gets straightened out."

"*You've* decided?" She half-laughed, then sobered when she recognized the determination in his stance. "What the hell was that little speech you just delivered about giving me room to run things my way?"

"When it quiets down around here and I'm sure you're out of danger, you can call all the shots you like. Until then, I'm not letting you out of my sight unless Willie's with you."

"I don't believe this!"

"Believe it," he said, striding back across the room like he owned it. He picked the container of dusting powder up off her dressing table and tossed it to her. "Make sure you pack this, okay? I like the way it smells on you."

Clutching the powder against her breast, she shot him a lethal glare. "You can go to hell. I'm not going anywhere with you."

He sighed with exaggerated patience. "Pay attention to what I'm about to tell you, Amanda. If the other incidents didn't convince you, the fire has got to tell you that you've got a major problem. Like it or not, you have to face the fact that someone's got it in for you."

She stubbornly held her ground.

Undaunted, he continued. "Now, this is the way it's going to be until we figure out what's going on. You go *nowhere*, you do *nothing*, without me or Willie by your side."

"But—"

A shake of his head cut off her protest. "You can sputter until hell freezes over. I don't care. And I don't give a damn if you like the arrangement or not. From now on, you've got a second shadow. Either Willie or I are going to be on you like spots on a ladybug. Now pack a bag, Sunshine. Oh, and make sure you throw in that thing you're wearing too."

Her scathing reply was cut off by a sharp rap on her bedroom door. Jesse opened it to Willie's worried face.

"Fire marshal's here, Jesse. He's got a lot of questions."

"He's not the only one," Jesse said, slipping out of the room. Poking his head back in, he issued his final warning. "If you're not out in five minutes, I'll be back in to get you . . . dressed or not."

A smart poker player knows when to fold and when to cover all bets. Amanda considered herself a smart player. She had to be, she thought, if she was going to get through this. Judging by the way her body had reacted to Jesse's skilled but aborted love-making, she didn't have a chance in hell of winning the game. But now wasn't the time to call his bluff. In the mood he was in, she knew he wouldn't stop at cheating to win.

So, like a smart player, she folded, and packed a bag . . . a small one. She didn't intend to play it his way for long.

True to his word, Jesse was waiting right outside her door, when Amanda stepped out of her room, dressed in her working clothes. Snagging the duffel from her hand, Jesse unzipped it, riffled through her jeans and shirts, scowled at her utilitarian under-things, then slipped back into her room. When he came out, a corner of her silk kimono peeked out of the hastily closed zipper and the scent of her dusting powder wafted up from inside the bag.

She drilled him a blistering look. His rebuttal was a full-throated chuckle as he hauled her up against him and dropped a smacking kiss on the top of her head.

"I think I know what your problem is, Sunshine. That ugly underwear is repressing your natural in-stincts and urges. We've *got* to get rid of it."

Had they not reached the front door at that partic-ular moment and come face-to-face with Willie and Fire Marshal Rawlings, Amanda would have told him what he could do with his seedy theory and his own underwear in graphic, if not ladylike, terms.

"Hello, Jack," Jesse said, releasing Amanda and extending his hand to the fire marshal. "I don't suppose you've got anything for us."

Jack Rawlings was a stocky, barrel-chested man of about fifty. He was also a neighboring rancher and a friend of the Kincannons for many years. His position as fire marshal was a part-time obligation that he undertook with as much diligence as he did his own ranch's responsibilities. Shaking his head, he fell into step with the trio as they headed for the ranch house.

"Sorry, Jesse," Rawlings said, whipping off his hat to smooth his thick shock of graying hair back from his forehead. "This one's got me stumped. Whoever was responsible for that fire knew what he was doing."

Amanda stopped dead. "*Who*, not *what*? You mean you've ruled out the possibility of an accident?"

At her stunned expression, Rawlings looked quickly at Jesse. After receiving a solemn nod from the younger man, he elaborated. "I'm afraid so, Amanda. All the evidence we've come up with proves the fire was deliberately set. And the damnedest thing is, whoever did it left more than enough clues to make sure anyone would know it was arson. It's almost like he's trying to get caught."

"Or like he wants to make sure Amanda knows the fire was meant for her," Jesse added, meeting Amanda's pensive stare.

Rawlings shrugged his broad shoulders. "Whatever the reason, they meant business. You're lucky you didn't lose the whole barn."

They reached the main house and curtailed conversation until the four of them were settled around the kitchen table with mugs of coffee.

Rawlings fidgeted uncomfortably in his chair. "Forgive me, Amanda, but I've got to ask. You're not in any . . . ah, trouble, are you?"

"Trouble?"

"Word travels, honey. I've heard about the problems you've been having. One or two of the incidents could be chalked up as accidents . . . *if* it had ended there. But it hasn't, and now this fire is too much to ignore. Somebody's got it in for you. I need to know if you know the reason why."

As she simply gazed at him in puzzlement, he continued. "You were gone a long time, Amanda. Lived in the city. There are ten kinds of temptation there that a woman who grew up on an isolated ranch might be inclined to get caught up in. Could it be you stepped over the wrong line and now the past is catching up with you?"

Willie, who'd been silent up until then, blasted Rawlings with a look that would have sent a lesser man into apoplexy. "Why you sumbitch," he swore, whipping his toothpick out of his mouth. "You got no call to accuse this girl of wrong doin'. You oughta be ashamed of yourself. You knew her daddy and her momma too. I ain't never heard of such a lame-brained, lop-eared—"

"Willie," Amanda cut in, smiling for the first time since this entire fiasco began. She covered Willie's leathery hand with hers and squeezed her champion's fingers tightly. "It's all right. Jack is just doing his job. He's got to explore all possible angles."

"Even so," Jesse said, "you're looking in the wrong gopher hole on this one, Jack. Amanda didn't bring this problem with her. I'd bet money on it."

"Amanda?" Jack asked doggedly, if apologetically.

"No, Jack. No drugs, no gambling debts, if that's what you're thinking. Sorry. I'm afraid the most exciting thing that ever happened to me was that I won a five-dollar pot at keno one night about three years ago. My first and only brush with lady luck."

"No boyfriend left behind with a grudge?" Jack asked, ignoring Willie's scowl.

Amanda fought to keep her gaze from straying to Jesse, who she sensed was watching her carefully. "No boyfriend."

The scrape of Jesse's chair against the floor brought her head up. He pushed away from the table and tunneled his hands through his hair.

"This is getting us nowhere, Jack," he said in frustration.

After taking a slow swallow of his coffee, Jack tried another angle. "All right then, what about here? Can you think of anyone you've run into since you've been back who has a grudge against you?"

There was no stopping her gaze from connecting with Jesse's this time. He was leaning against the counter, his arms crossed over his chest, his expression brooding. He waited in silence for her reply.

"No," she said finally, unable to look him in the eye. "No one."

"No one but me and my sister, Lucy," Jesse corrected her soberly. "Tell him, Sunshine," he prompted, meeting her troubled look with a smile that wasn't really a smile.

Amanda drew a deep breath. "Lucy wasn't too happy when Walt put me in charge. She's been pretty vocal about her feelings."

"And Jesse?" Jack asked, lifting a brow.

Jesse answered for her. "And Jesse couldn't give a damn about what the old man decided to do with his ranch. Only I don't think Amanda's quite convinced of that."

"Appears to me that Jesse would have nothing to gain by burning down his own barn," Jack said tactfully, before Amanda could respond to the faint hurt she heard in Jesse's voice. Whatever else she might think of him, she knew he'd never try to harm her. "Willie," Jack went on, "you got any ideas?"

Willie shook his head, his stony stare telegraphing the fact that he hadn't yet forgiven Jack for his slur against Amanda's character.

"What about Jake?" Amanda asked carefully.

All three heads turned toward her.

"Smiling Jake?" Willie asked skeptically.

"He doesn't seem to approve of me."

Jesse pushed himself away from the counter, spun a kitchen chair around, and straddled it. "He is an odd one, isn't he? Always skulking around corners, never has much to say. What do you know about him, Willie?"

Willie sat silent for a moment, scratching his jaw in long, thoughtful strokes. Finally, he snorted. "Well, when it comes right down to it, not a lot, I guess. I never thought about it much, to tell you the truth."

"Where'd he come from?" Rawlings asked.

"Who knows? Near as I can figure, he's been around these parts for ten, fifteen years, maybe. Worked on pert near every ranch in the county at one time or another, but seemed to kinda settle in when he lit here. Seems like I remember he worked for Conn Warren just afore he signed on here last fall." Willie gulped some coffee and continued. "Simpleminded soul. Don't have much to say. Now that I think on it, I believe one of the boys told me he used to be a bronc rider. Lit on his head one too many times. That's what made him so slowlike and kinda dim-witted. Son of a gun can sit a rank horse like no man I ever seen, though, I can tell you that."

Rawlings drained his coffee cup and stood. "I think maybe I'll have a little talk with Jake."

Jesse pushed himself to his feet. "I'll come with you. Willie, you stay with Amanda."

She groaned. "Dammit, Jess, I don't need—"

"We've been over this before. I'm not leaving you alone."

"Jess, this is ridiculous. Willie has work to do. He can't trail me everywhere I go. It's not fair to him. It's not fair to me. And if I don't go into town for groceries soon—"

Jesse cut her off again with a pointing finger and a belligerent scowl. "Enough! I'm not going to argue with you about this again. As far as the supplies go, make a list. Carolyn has been itching for an excuse to get off the ranch for a little while. She'll be more than happy to pick up whatever you need in town." Firmly settling his Stetson on his head, he dismissed Amanda's steel-eyed stare and turned to a very quiet Willie. "She gives you any static, you paddle her sweet little ass."

With that, he stormed out the door, a grinning fire marshal in tow.

Five

"Once upon a time," Amanda murmured as she reacquainted herself with the beautiful room Jesse had designated as hers. Ice-blue antique satin draped the windows and the bed. A pristine white eyelet duster skimmed the floor around the big four-poster. Here and there, wispy touches of femininity made the room a princesslike fantasy.

Yes, once upon a time she'd dreamed of a prince's kiss and the chance to sleep like a princess in this room.

She didn't feel much like a princess that night, though. She felt more like a prisoner. Oh, she had free run of the house. Jesse had insisted on that. But thanks to her own stubbornness, it was barely seven o'clock and unless she wanted to eat a plate full of self-righteous crow, she was stuck there for the night with nothing to do but stare at four white walls.

She was alone with her childhood fantasies and her adult fears. Yet for all the unease she felt over the fire and the danger she apparently was in, all she could think about was Jesse.

He stuck in her thoughts like a seasoned rider to

an unsettled mount. Held her captive in his house while another woman slept down the hall in his bed.

Frustrated, confused, she threw a pillow across the room and swore for what seemed like the hundredth time that day. "Damn you, Jess Kincannon! What are you doing to me?"

As if he'd been waiting outside the room for just such an oath, Jesse flung open the door and stormed in.

"Come on," he said, grabbing her wrist and dragging her to her feet.

Something in his eyes, something hard and a little frightening, told her to hold her tongue. Stunned by his inexplicable anger, she didn't even protest as he hauled her outside and into the pickup.

Less than a minute later she wished she had dug in her heels and stayed put. He squealed out of the drive like a madman.

"Jesse," she cried breathlessly as they flew over a pothole on the poorly graded dirt road. "If you don't slow down, you're going to get us both killed!"

Clenched-jawed, tight-lipped, Jesse checked his watch. He swore explicitly, then skidded around a curve and onto the main highway, where he slammed the accelerator to the floor.

"For God's sake, Jesse! Can't you at least tell me what I'm going to die for? Jess, please . . . what's going on?"

The fear in her voice must have finally gotten through to him. Relaxing his white-knuckled grip on the steering wheel, he backed off slightly on the speed.

"The sheriff's office called," he said. "Carolyn's been in an accident."

The anguish Amanda heard in his voice tore at her. "Oh, Jess. I'm sorry. Is she . . . How is she?"

"I don't know. All they'd tell me is that she was

conscious when they found her and that they took her to Memorial."

"How . . . what happened? Did they tell you that?"

His grip on the wheel tightened. Very briefly, he met Amanda's eyes. What she saw in his ice-blue gaze sent a chill slithering down the length of her spine.

"She told a deputy that someone deliberately forced her off the road."

"Deliberately . . . forced her?" Amanda repeated in stunned disbelief. Her heart lurched violently as the magnitude of what he'd said slammed into her. "Oh God, Jess . . ." The awful truth tightened like a knot around her throat.

He reached out and squeezed her hand. "Yeah, baby," he said, and completed her thought aloud. "She was driving your car."

A sinking wave of nausea rolled over Amanda as she clearly remembered Carolyn obligingly taking the grocery list and the keys to Amanda's compact, then breezing out the kitchen door right after the evening meal.

Amanda closed her eyes. Her head fell back against the seat as the panic, the fear, and the guilt engulfed her. "It was supposed to be me. Whoever ran her off the road thought it was me."

Relief swept through Amanda as she listened to the emergency room doctor confer with Jesse.

". . . She was a lucky woman," the young resident was saying as he consulted Carolyn's chart. "The cast will need to stay on her wrist for six weeks, but it was a clean break and should heal completely. The skull X rays look good too. Only a slight concussion. She's got a nasty lump on her head, though, and a beauty of a shiner. She'll have a hell of a headache for a couple of days, but other than that, she's fine. Lucky woman," he repeated. "You can go in and see her now if you'd like, but don't stay too long, okay?"

Jesse clasped the doctor's hand firmly, then headed for the door he'd indicated. Amanda followed behind.

The room was dimly lit. Carolyn lay with her casted arm resting across her lap, her face turned toward the wall. Her left eye was dismally swollen and discolored. A pristine white bandage held her blonde hair back from her face. When she heard the door open, she slowly turned her head toward it and tried for a valiant smile.

She looked pale and fragile in the diluted light, and at that moment, Amanda admired Carolyn a whole lot.

Jesse's shoulders sagged when he looked at her. A low, strangled moan echoed from deep in his throat.

"Hey, Jesse," Carolyn murmured.

Jesse walked across the room. With infinite care, he lowered the side rail on the hospital bed and settled a hip on the mattress. "What some women won't do to get a little attention," he said gruffly.

"You know me," Carolyn responded, her words slow, her voice thick. "Always out for a new thrill."

Amanda hung back by the door. Her heart ached in the face of Jesse's obvious feelings for this woman. Tears of loss, of guilt, crowded the back of her eyes.

"You look like hell," he said with a gentle smile. He let out a huge sigh, then shook his head. "Your old man is going to skin me alive and hang me out to dry when he sees how I took care of you."

Carolyn's bravado faltered. "Will you call him for me, Jesse?" she asked, a sob punctuating her words.

"Sure, baby." He smoothed a hand over her hair. "I'll call him tonight, okay? The miserable old bull will move heaven and earth to get here. You wait and see. He'll be tearing this hospital apart by morning."

Carolyn rewarded him with a watery smile. "I have to stay all night for observation, but they'll let me leave first thing in the morning." She paused to lick dry lips. "Think you can get me out of here and back to the ranch before he shows up? I'd kind of like to keep his little blowup between friends."

Jesse nodded. "Whatever you want." He lifted her uninjured hand to his mouth. "I'm sorry," he whispered hoarsely against her pale fingers.

"I know." Carolyn closed her eyes as the pain-killers they'd given her took hold. "See you at first light, Jesse."

Amanda watched in aching silence as Jesse lowered Carolyn's hand to her side. "First light," he repeated, and sat with her for the moment it took her to slip into sleep.

Swallowing the lump in her throat, Amanda eased quietly from the room. As she stood numbly in the antiseptic corridor, the knowledge that it should have been her lying in that bed pounded against her.

A hollow-eyed Jesse walked out of Carolyn's room a minute later. He sagged against the wall and closed his eyes. Unable to witness his pain, Amanda started to walk away.

His hand reached out to snag hers. He pulled her up against him, wrapped her in his arms, and held on tight.

Until she felt his solid strength against her, Amanda hadn't known how much she'd needed this from him. She clung to him. "I'm so sorry, Jess," she whispered against his chest. "It—it could have been me. It *should* have been me," she stated adamantly as she knotted her fists in his shirt. "She . . . could have been killed."

Jesse's heartbeat thundered against her ear like an echo of her words. For a long, calming moment, he simply held her. Then his embrace became fierce, his possessive hold telling her everything she needed to hear—that it scared the hell out of him, too, that he didn't blame her for what happened. That he cared.

Tilting her face up to his with the slightest pressure of his thumbs under her jaw, he asked, "You okay?"

She nodded.

"Come on then. Let's see what we can find out at the sheriff's office, then go have a look at your car."

Tucking her tightly against his side, he headed down the corridor.

Amanda had to give Carolyn credit. She was a hell of a lot tougher than she looked. Truth was, when Jesse brought her back to the ranch around nine o'clock the next morning, Amanda was a little in awe of Carolyn's quiet grit.

Jesse made a big fuss about carrying her into the house. Carolyn wouldn't have any of it. She insisted he quit acting like an overprotective parent and let her walk on her own two feet. "The general consensus," she scolded good-naturedly, "is that a broken wrist doesn't affect one's ability to walk."

Amanda watched this affectionate byplay with mixed emotions, and drew mixed conclusions. Jesse's concern seemed less loverlike than parental. At the very least, he was acting fraternal. Leaning a shoulder against the door frame as Jesse helped Carolyn into her bedroom—a bedroom that was at the farthest end of the hall from Jesse's and looked very lived in—Amanda felt herself warming toward this woman she wanted to dislike.

At the same time she was absorbing and weighing this discovery, Carolyn turned and sent her a beseeching look. It was a fleeting glance, but it held a wealth of appeal. And it was the first step toward friendship between them.

"Jesse," Amanda said as she stepped between him and Carolyn, effectively squeezing him aside, "if you don't back off, you're going to kill this woman with kindness. All this nervous fussing is tiring her. Go," she said, shooing him out of the room. When he just stood there, she repeated herself more forcefully. "Go. She's a big girl and perfectly capable of letting you know if she needs anything."

"I'm all right, Jesse. Really," Carolyn said, her smile pinched as she eased down on the bed.

Jesse backed out of the room wearing a scowl of sheer male intolerance. Ignoring his stormy look, Amanda closed the door in his face, realizing as she did that she'd just crossed a line of some sort where Carolyn was concerned.

"Thanks," Carolyn said.

A little uncomfortable with this unlikely camaraderie, Amanda turned and gave the other woman a sketchy smile. "He means well," she said in Jesse's defense, then in the next breath wondered why she'd defended him.

If Carolyn noticed Amanda's confusion, she didn't comment. Instead, she picked up a hand mirror from the bedside table and studied her reflection.

"I had a shiner like that once," Amanda said sympathetically. She walked to the foot of the bed and sat down. "In another day or two, you'll be able to cover it with makeup."

Tears welled up in Carolyn's eyes. "I haven't got a day or two. Hoyt will more than likely be here within the next couple of hours. I don't want him to see me like this. Will you help me?"

Hoyt? Amanda repeated silently. She called her father Hoyt? "I'm sure he won't care about anything except that you're all right. Parents are like that. They—"

"Parents?"

"Sure," Amanda said helpfully. "Your father will be so glad to see you, he'll look right past that eye."

"My father? My father's coming?" Carolyn asked with such puzzlement, Amanda suspected her concussion was worse than the doctor had diagnosed.

"Don't you remember? Last night, you asked Jesse to call him."

Carolyn's face went blank for a split second before a grin put the life back into it. "Amanda . . . Jesse didn't call my father. He called my husband."

"Your . . ." Amanda swallowed, unable to say it. "Your husband?"

Carolyn nodded. "The one who's going to hang Jesse out to dry when he sees me like this."

Amanda took a deep breath as the light dawned. With the light came relief, then elation. Close on its heels, though, was a thunderous, blood-boiling anger.

For the life of her, Amanda didn't know how she could be so angry and so elated at the same time. As she gently helped Carolyn dress and fix her hair and makeup, Carolyn filled her in on the reason she'd come to the Flying K.

"Hoyt's the kind of man you have to know to truly love, and even then hate runs a close second."

Hoyt Haggerty, Amanda thought. She could hardly believe it. Carolyn's husband was a country legend, akin to Willie Nelson and the lone wolf, Waylon Jennings. And Carolyn loved him. And Jesse was both Carolyn's and Hoyt's friend, not Carolyn's lover. And Jesse was lower than pond scum for not telling her the entire story.

"Anyway," Carolyn continued as Amanda carefully applied powder around her swollen eye, "he was pushing himself too hard. The harder Hoyt pushes, the more withdrawn he becomes. He drinks too much, works too hard. Before Jesse left Tennessee to come here, he tried to talk some sense into Hoyt. It didn't work. Nothing did. I couldn't sit by and watch it any longer, so I called Jesse and he agreed to let me stay here."

Carolyn paused to study Amanda's handiwork, and Amanda keyed in on her comment about Tennessee. So that was where Jesse had picked up his faint Southern accent.

"Jesse loves Hoyt too," Carolyn continued, apparently needing to talk as much as Amanda needed to listen. "We figured that if I just disappeared for a while, maybe it would shock Hoyt into coming to his senses."

Amanda was just feeling brave enough to ask how the three of them had come to be friends, when she heard shouts outside in the hall.

Carolyn's gaze flew to Amanda's. "Oh, Lord. He's here. How do I look?"

Amanda couldn't help but smile at the notion that this beautiful woman could truly be worried about her appearance. "Let's put it this way," she said. "He's going to take one look at you and turn to mush."

The door burst open just then and a bull of a man barreled into the room. Amanda jumped back from the bed, instantly alert to the dark anger and overpowering physical presence of Hoyt Haggerty. For a moment, but only for a moment, she experienced a thread of fear for Carolyn. Then magically, the sinister, almost piratical features of the country star softened when his gaze landed on his wife.

The love, the raging fear, and the big man's panic were all relayed in that one poignant look. He crossed swiftly to the bed and knelt down on one knee beside it. With infinite care, he took Carolyn's hand in his and held it to his heart. For the space of several heartbeats, Amanda stood transfixed by the love that flowed between husband and wife.

With as little sound as she could manage, she tiptoed to the doorway where Jesse stood ready to intervene.

"Come on," she whispered, closing the door behind her. "They need to be alone."

Jesse shook his head. "I don't know—"

"That's right, Kincannon," she said vehemently. "You don't know. Anything!" She stormed down the hall and out the front door.

She was halfway to the stallion barn before Jesse caught up with her. "Amanda!" he yelled, grabbing her.

"Leave me alone, you jerk!" She wrenched her arm free from his hold and kept on walking.

"I don't know what you're so fired up about," he said, falling in step with her long strides.

"That's because you're as dumb as a fence post and as insensitive as that old jack mule my dad used to have."

"What's that supposed to mean?" he snarled, grabbing her arm again and spinning her around to face him.

Furious with him for all the torment she'd gone through, thinking she was falling for him while he had another woman in his bed, she swung at him, just because it felt so good to do it. He caught her arm midswing and pinned it behind her back.

"Dammit, Amanda, you swing at me again and I swear, I won't—"

"Won't what? Won't hesitate to swing back? It wouldn't surprise me if you did! But just because you're bigger than me, Kincannon, doesn't mean you can control me."

"Like hell, I can't!" Snaring both arms in his big

hands, he hauled her up against him and held her so she couldn't move.

Amanda fought to ignore the heat and the hardness of him as their bodies fused together beneath the warm Montana sun. "That's your answer to everything, isn't it?" she shouted. "If you can't make them believe a lie, you overpower them with your caveman tactics and then put the moves on until they're panting and hot for you."

"Amanda, you're not talking sense."

"And *you* weren't talking at all! She had a husband. A husband, dammit! Why couldn't you have just told me instead of—" She stopped, too embarrassed to finish.

"Instead of what, Amanda?" he asked, drawing her tighter against him.

Amanda had to arch her neck back to look at him. "Instead of making me think what I did."

"If I remember right, I tried to explain. Several times. You weren't having any of it."

Practically breathing fire, she flared back, "I wasn't having any of your fumbling sexual advances, either, but that didn't stop you from trying, did it?"

In a moment of stunning awareness, Amanda suddenly realized where they were and that she was shouting at the top of her lungs. She looked around quickly. Several hat-covered heads turned back to the business of restructuring the burned-out barn. She wanted to crawl into a hole and die of embarrassment.

"Let me go," she muttered between clenched teeth.

With a great show of care, Jesse released her. Holding his hands clear of his body, he backed a safe distance away. "If you're finished making a spectacle of yourself," he said reasonably, "let's go back inside and talk this through like two adults."

Her snort would have made Willie proud. "That would be a real stretch. *You* talking like an adult."

"Amanda," he warned.

"Go to hell, Kincannon. I'm not going anywhere with you. I'm going for a ride." She turned on her heel and headed for the stallion barn.

A bony hand snagged Jesse's arm and stopped him from following.

"Why don't I go with her, Jesse?" Willie said carefully. "Don't appear like now's the time for you to plead your case. Let the girl ride off a little steam."

Jesse hung his hands on his hips and watched her go. "All right," he said with considerable reluctance. "But stick with her, Willie."

Willie tugged his hat down low on his forehead. "Like bad breath on a badger, boss," he promised with a salty grin. "Now, don't worry. Ol' Willie won't let her outa his sight."

Six

"I ain't never in my life heard so many doors slammed in such a short time," Willie remarked over his coffee two mornings later.

Tina Rodriguez, back to her duties only that morning, was all ears as Willie, her longtime confidant and friend filled her in on the goings-on during her absence. Like Willie, Tina had been with the Kincannons almost from day one. She was a plump, graying widow who'd lost her husband many years ago and had since adopted the Kincannon ranch and its crew as her extended family. She dried the last of the breakfast dishes and joined Willie at the table.

"I felt it the minute I walked into this kitchen," she said as she smoothed an errant strand of hair back into the bun she wore at the nape of her neck. "There're ten kinds of tension sifting through the walls of this old house. Now I know why."

Willie grinned. "I'd say you came back just in time. It's bound to get hotter around here yet. What, with Jesse sticking like glue to Amanda and her refusing to look at him, let alone speak to him, something's bound to blow soon. Ol' Jesse never looses his cool with her, but he's getting crankier than a long-tailed cat in a room full a rockin' chairs."

Tina smiled briefly, then sobered. "This business about someone trying to hurt Amanda . . . I don't like it. It doesn't make any sense."

Willie's chest rose with his tired sigh. "At least nothing's happened for the past few days. I gotta figure that Jesse's right about keeping Amanda in our sights. Seems to have put a stop to things in that quarter. And now that you're back, there'll be one more set of eyes to watch over her."

A groan from the kitchen doorway brought their heads up.

"Tina," Amanda pleaded as she walked into the kitchen in her work clothes, "if you care about me at all, you won't let them enlist you too. I'm beginning to feel like an animal trapped in a cage."

"Make that a viper," Jesse muttered as he strode into the kitchen behind her, his boot heels thumping on the oak floor. "With fangs bared."

Ignoring Jesse and his remark, Amanda reached for the coffeepot. When Jesse grabbed an empty mug and set it beside hers on the counter, she blithely filled her own, then returned the pot to the stove.

Jesse did his tenth slow burn of the morning as he watched her sit down at the table. "Why, thank you, Amanda," he said with saccharine sweetness. "So nice of you to pour." He filled his mug with a great show of patience and, crossing his legs at the ankles, leaned against the counter.

"Nice to have you back, Tina," he said, saluting her with his mug. "Maybe now a man can look forward to a decent meal around here again. Not to mention that there's nothing prettier than a woman's smiling face and sweet disposition."

Tina flushed with embarrassment.

Willie cleared his throat chastisingly.

If Amanda noticed Jesse's blatant put-down, she didn't show it as she turned a bright smile to Tina. "You didn't put away those pictures of your granddaughter, did you, Tina? I didn't get a good look at them before breakfast."

Only too happy to show off her grandchild and to ease a little of the tension in the room, Tina rushed to the pantry to get her purse and retrieve the snapshots. When she came back, the kitchen was empty except for Amanda.

"They decided they could trust me to stay with you for a little while," Amanda said when Tina looked around in surprise. "And frankly, I welcome the reprieve. Jesse's acting like my jailer."

Tina fixed her with a stern look. "Jesse cares very much for you."

"Jesse cares about Jesse," Amanda said flatly, ignoring the pang of pain those words brought her. "He always has. He just doesn't want any more trouble cropping up at the Flying K."

"You are truly blind if you can't see how he looks at you."

"Oh, you mean the I-want-to-get-you-in-my-bed look?"

"It's more than his bed he wants you in. The man has one of the worst cases of smitten I've ever seen. And feeding hungry ranch hands for half of my life, I've seen my share of cases."

Amanda stared thoughtfully out the window. "He hasn't been honest with me, Tina."

"He's a man," Tina said as if that explained everything. "Sometimes they just can't help it."

Feeling her belligerence slipping, Amanda tried to shore it up. "He made a fool of me."

"So now you're going to be a bigger fool by refusing to forgive him?"

"He hasn't asked for my forgiveness."

"It's not likely that he will," Tina said, then added with a sage smile, "most men just don't have it in them."

Amanda's eyes sparkled with newly kindled fire. "And that's supposed to make it all right?"

"It is if you want to be with him."

"I don't want to be with him. I don't even know him."

"You know him."

Amanda shook her head in exasperation. "Knowing Jesse and understanding him are two entirely different roads. I don't understand Jesse the man any better than I did Jesse the child."

"Yes, you do."

Amanda frowned at Tina, irritated by the woman's persistence—and by her insight. Tina was right. Amanda did understand Jesse. She always had. He was a rebel and a maverick because he'd learned early to protect himself. He'd encouraged his own dissension rather than suffer his father's rejection. "Cutting out the middleman," he used to call it.

Amanda fought the softening she felt around her heart. Just because she understood Jesse didn't mean he'd ever love her. "He's secretive and evasive," she said, as much to convince herself as Tina. "I don't even know where he lives, what he does when he isn't here, how many women he keeps on his silver string."

"Have you bothered to ask?"

Amanda buried her gaze in her coffee.

"I didn't think so." Tina sighed. "You have changed, child. The Amanda I used to know was self-confident and believed in herself."

"I still believe. I believe I'd be a fool to think a man like Jesse could want someone like me for anything more than a temporary diversion. Besides, I've played that part before. I didn't like it."

"It doesn't always have to turn out that way. Besides, what feels worse?" Tina asked quietly. "Foolish or frustrated?"

Amanda looked down at her hands, then up at Tina. Once again, the older woman was right. It wasn't like Amanda to be so limp-wristed. She could thank Todd for that. But she could thank Jesse for the frustration she'd felt for days. It was wearing a little thin.

"Foolish or frustrated," she mused aloud. "Some choice. I guess I'll have to take a little more time deciding. In the meantime, at least I can take comfort in the fact that I'm not the only one feeling frustrated."

Tina laughed. "Jesse does have a bit of a reined-in look about him, doesn't he?"

A slow, utterly feminine smile curved Amanda's mouth. "You noticed that, did you?"

"Oh, I noticed. And I think Jesse may be right. You do have your fangs bared. Just remember this, Amanda. It's fine to make him squirm for a little while . . . but don't push it too long if you decide you don't want to lose him. A man has his pride and it's so much more bruisable than a woman's."

Amanda could have told Tina that she knew all about bruises. But she didn't, and this time she wasn't so sure Tina was right.

The Haggertys left that same afternoon. Standing in the drive beside Hoyt's rented car, Jesse and Amanda watched as Hoyt stuffed Carolyn's bags into the trunk, then carefully tucked Carolyn into the front seat.

When he was satisfied she was comfortable, he turned to Jesse. "I owe you one, man," he said solemnly, extending his hand.

"Just see to it there's no need for you to owe me again." Jesse grasped his friend's hand in a hard grip. "She's a hell of a woman. Take care of her."

Amanda observed the exchange with newfound respect for Jesse. Seeing the two men together the past few days had made her realize how close they were. Hoyt was considerably older than both Carolyn and Jesse. She sensed a father-friend relationship between the two men and understood that Jesse had put everything on the line when he'd taken Carolyn in. Fortunately, it had paid off for the Haggertys.

"Ah, look," Hoyt stammered, his emotions obviously near the surface, "if we don't get going, we'll miss our flight. Thanks again, Jess," he said earnestly.

Jesse nodded, then bent to give Carolyn a gentle kiss. "That gnarly old bastard gives you any more grief, you know who to call."

Carolyn caressed his jaw with a shaking hand, then thanked him with a smile that told anyone who saw it how happy she was. Amanda watched the car pull away, feeling a bittersweet longing for just a taste of that kind of love.

The Haggertys hadn't been gone a week when Amanda received a letter from Carolyn. She took it to the blue room after dinner and settled down on the bed to read it.

> *Amanda:*
>
> *I don't know how to begin so I'll just plunge in feetfirst. First, I must apologize for imposing on your hospitality and for stomping all over your feelings. Believe me, I wanted to clear the air regarding my relationship with Jesse, but he wouldn't let*

*me. He's stubborn that way. Trust is so very
important to him. He wanted you to trust
him based on his actions rather than his
past. A very male trait, wouldn't you say,
and not necessarily a good one? But the
bottom line is, you should trust him. He's a
very special man. Something else you
should trust are your own feelings where
Jesse is concerned. Yes, Amanda, they
show. If you're as smart as I think you are,
you'll do the right thing.*

*My injuries are healing. So is my mar-
riage. I've never seen Hoyt so attentive.
Give my love to Jesse. Until we meet again,*

Carolyn . . . .

Amanda folded the letter and tucked it back into its
envelope. Rolling onto her stomach, she mulled over
Carolyn's message. Carolyn had thought enough of
her—and of Jesse to interfere. And truly, that was
the sole reason for the letter. Carolyn was trying to
undo some of the harm Jesse himself had done.
Interesting, Amanda thought, that so many people
had such vastly different impressions of Jesse Kincannon than she. The Haggertys, Tina, even Willie
thought the man could do no wrong.

That last thought niggled until she found herself
reassessing, reevaluating. Was Jesse right? Was it
the sins of the child she couldn't forgive? Or was it
the sins of another man she was unfairly pinning on
Jesse? Todd's betrayal had definitely nurtured her
feelings of inadequacy.

She rose slowly from the bed and approached the
dresser. Its mirror reflected freshly scrubbed cheeks,
a hastily manufactured French braid, her standard
flannel work shirt and old faded jeans. "Tom Sawyer

could love this face," she muttered in disgust. "But Jesse Kincannon?"

Touching a hand to her throat, she searched for the woman Jesse insisted he wanted. No vamp here. Yes, she had a slim, curving figure, but she fell far short of voluptuous. Actually, she decided, looking over her shoulder for a rear view, she didn't fall *that* short. Her hips were trim but nicely rounded. Her breasts, though not large, were firm and high and filled out the pockets of her shirt well enough.

"What kind of a woman could feel appealing in these clothes?" she asked her reflection, still searching for what Jesse saw beneath the denim and flannel that she'd forgotten she had. "And that hair. How long has it been since you even tried to make yourself attractive?"

Too long. Striking while the fire was hot inside her, she marched out of the bedroom to the living room, where she knew she'd find Jesse and Willie relaxing over a cup of coffee.

"I've changed my mind," she said abruptly, not quite able to meet Jesse's eyes.

He shot a bewildered glance at Willie who merely shrugged.

"What would this mind change be about, Amanda?" Jesse asked suspiciously.

"About going into town for the evening. Do you two still want to go?" She directed her question at Willie.

Willie scratched his jaw while Jesse made a great fuss refolding the evening newspaper.

"Seems to me," Willie began laconically, "that a night on the town at the Lady Slipper would be a damn fine way to shake off some of the tension that's settled in around this ranch lately."

"That was why I suggested it this morning," Jesse said, sounding testy.

Amanda knew he was still stinging from her earlier

refusal. Frankly, she didn't blame him. As of that evening, she vowed silently, her attitude toward Jesse would swing one hundred and eighty degrees. After all, as Tina had said, she didn't want to lose him. Not before she'd had him all to herself for at least a little while.

"I'm sorry I refused your invitation earlier," she said. "I do think it's a good idea." She bit her lip to keep from laughing at the distrustful scowl Jesse threw her.

"Okay," he said finally. "Let's do it. I'm just stir crazy enough that I'll chance it."

"Great," she said with more enthusiasm than she'd mustered in days. "I'll be ready in an hour."

Both men sat perfectly still, their brows beetled in thought, as she swept gaily out of the room.

"What the hell do you suppose she's up to?" Jesse asked Willie as he watched her go.

"I'm sure I wouldn't know. But if I were you, I'd watch myself tonight. That little kitty might be purring real sweet right now, but I'd wager before the night's over, she'll be sharpening her claws in your back if you so much as cross over the wrong line."

"That little kitty," Jesse said slowly, "has used me for a scratching board for too damn long. Anybody draws blood tonight, it's going to be me."

Employing some of the tricks she'd used to help make Carolyn presentable for Hoyt, Amanda deftly applied her makeup. Just enough blush to emphasize her high cheekbones. Just enough shadow to enlarge her dark eyes, which were crystal bright with anticipation. And finally, just enough lip gloss to mold her lower lip into a full, sultry pout. The image flashed through her mind of Jesse's mouth making love to her own, his tanned, callused fingertips caressing her bare breast.

Her heart raced . . . with excitement, with the realization that without making a conscious decision, she intended to cross a line that night. Not a line. She intended to leap over a gorge. She looked herself straight in the eye. "Once you cross over, there'll be no going back. Not with Jesse."

Shivering sensuously, she ignored the warnings that glared like red lights in her head. She'd spent too many sleepless nights remembering the passion of Jesse's kisses, the sensual demand of his body pressing her to the bed, the torturous yearning he'd made her feel when she'd wanted nothing more than to hate him.

Fairly buzzing with reckless energy, she styled her hair in loose, feathery sweeps away from her face. Stripping off her robe, she treated herself to another dusting of the bath powder Jesse loved.

Her expectant high took a bit of a dive when she opened her bureau drawer. When she'd left the city for the ranch, she'd been determined to make a clean break. Her silk and lace underthings hadn't been even vaguely suited to life on a working ranch. Except for the silk kimono she couldn't bear to part with, every single dainty piece was now in the hands of her old roommate.

Longing for just one of her sexy teddies, Amanda stepped into her cotton briefs and tugged a U-neck undershirt over her head. But that night even the underwear Jesse scorned couldn't dampen her spirits. The high-cut jockey-style briefs hugged her hips like a lover's broad hands. The ribbed cotton undershirt felt slightly abrasive as she smoothed it over her breasts. Her nipples tightened, her breasts swelled, sensitized by erotic images of Jesse's mouth loving them.

By the time she'd buttoned and zipped herself into her skirt and blouse and approached the mirror, she liked how she felt. She liked what she saw too. And so would Jesse.

Her stone-washed denim skirt was full and feminine, falling about her hips in soft folds and ending at midcalf. The pale blue peasant blouse exposed her throat and upper chest, and if she chose, the curves of her shoulders. She chose.

Filled with a new confidence in herself as a woman, she slipped into soft kidskin boots of a pale buttery tan, then misted perfume behind each ear. On a stroke of sheer womanly intuition, she added a spritz between her breasts. Jesse may be a master at seduction, but she had her own kind of torture in mind for him that night.

It was then that it hit her. She was no schoolgirl preening for her first date. She was a woman, with a woman's wants. A woman's needs. Needs that went beyond the physical and cut straight to the heart. She needed Jesse Kincannon.

The thought was sobering, but it felt good to finally admit it. A fact was, after all, a fact, and realist that she was, Amanda recognized that certain facts could not be altered. The sun rose in the morning. The sky was blue. The mountains were high. Amanda loved Jesse. When he left her, she'd hurt.

Though the last and inevitable fact gave her pause, she didn't want to deal with it right then. Instead, filled more with a sense of adventure than with common sense, she swept out the bedroom door.

"Jesse Kincannon," she murmured in warning, "prepare to be knocked off your size-eleven feet."

But when she encountered a very subdued Jesse waiting in the living room, it was she who felt like her legs had been chopped out from under her.

She stopped just inside the door, barely capable of

breathing, let alone taking another step. He didn't notice her, so she took her fill of the picture he made sitting in a chair.

Jesse in faded denim and trail dust was a sight to make even the faintest heart clamor. Jesse the way he looked that night was an assault to every holy and unholy thought even the most committed celibate had ever entertained.

He still wore jeans, but these were newer, tighter, and if possible, made his sinewy legs seem even longer as they tapered down to boots much the color of her own. He'd traded his chambray shirt for a deep burgundy T-shirt that clung to his body like a desperate woman before disappearing beneath his belt. Over the shirt, he wore an unconstructed jacket of a rich chamois color, the sleeves pushed up to reveal his strong, tanned forearms.

He was undeniably male, unrepentantly beautiful. When he turned his head and saw her standing there, he unfolded himself in slow motion and reached for his Stetson.

Amanda had a fleeting notion that it would be criminal to cover his perfectly combed black hair, that until that moment she'd sworn was untamable. The thought fled with her breath when he settled the dun-colored hat on his head and completed the picture. Without a doubt, Jesse Kincannon was the most drop-dead gorgeous, the most irreverently sexy cowboy she'd ever seen.

Incredible, she thought, vaguely aware of Willie whistling his way into the room.

Willie stopped in his tracks when he spotted Amanda. "Well, I'll be rode hard and put away wet," he said after executing a double take worthy of a stand-up comic. "Sweet little Amanda," he muttered with undisguised affection. "Just look at her, Jesse. Damn, but she cleaned up good, didn't she?"

Willie's uncharacteristic, though nonetheless backdoor compliment earned a self-conscious smile from Amanda.

Jesse, on the other hand, seemed as spellbound as Willie. "Yeah," he agreed hoarsely, then cleared his throat. "Real good."

Dragging his gaze away from her, he turned to Willie and smothered a surprised grin. "You're looking pretty spiffy yourself, partner."

Willie smoothed a bony hand down the front of his new shirt. "I may not get out of the saddle too often these days, but don't you kid yourself, Jesse. This old cowpoke still knows how to attract hisself a few cows."

Jesse laughed. "Never doubted it for a minute. Come on, let's hit the road. Unless, of course, you plan on standing here jawing about your good looks all night."

"You know what I've always had a hankerin' to do?" Willie asked a bit hesitantly as they strolled outside together.

"What's that, Willie?" Jesse asked.

"Well, I rode my share of rank horses, sat many a John Deere tractor and a GMC truck, but I never"—he cast a quick, almost apologetic look toward Jesse's Porsche—"drove me anything like that machine there."

"You want to drive the Porsche?" Jesse asked with a grin. He fished the keys out of his pocket and tossed them to Willie. "Have at it."

At this point Amanda could have questioned her normally sedate foreman about his uncharacteristic lighthearted mood and his sudden penchant to drive a sports car. She had heard him say to Tina just the day before, "Why anyone of sound mind would want to waste good money on a shiny bucket of overpriced horsepower, when he could sit astride the real thing, is beyond my power of reason." Instead, she smiled and watched Willie make a great show of climbing behind the wheel.

She could have also pointed out that there was a logistics problem with seating three people in a two-seater sports car. She could have, but she didn't, even though the arrangement reeked of conspiracy.

Instead, she prepared to enjoy the ride. To enjoy Jesse. Finally. She settled herself on his lap in the passenger seat as if it were the most natural thing in the world for her to do.

And it was natural. His thighs were hard and strong beneath her bottom. His breath, where it grazed her throat, smelled minty and cool. As the miles passed, it became increasingly difficult for her to remember they weren't alone. The heat of his body and the scent of his skin stirred the woman within her to aching awareness. She thought of his wild, stolen kisses and wished for him to steal some more.

Jesse, it seemed, suffered neither from the cause nor the effect. Amanda might as well not have been in the car as he chatted nonstop to Willie about cattle and the price of good stock.

Fighting her irritation, she only grew more aware of the strong arms that held her. Her skin tingled. Her breast, where it pressed against his chest, felt heavy and hot.

Jesse shifted her in his lap like she were a bother-some sack of groceries and laughed at Willie's lead foot.

The shifting of bodies created greater intimacy. Lush new rivers of need sluiced through Amanda, cutting uncharted courses in her own sensuality. She felt willowy and winsome, ripe for Jesse's gentle caress.

He patted her bottom, made a glib, patronizing comment about the way she filled out her jeans, and told Willie he approved of a ranch manager with a healthy appetite.

By the time they roared into town, Amanda's new-found confidence had as much umph as a tire with a fast leak. Her anger, however, was building like a storm over the Rockies, gaining force as it hovered.

When Willie eased to a stop in the parking lot, Amanda couldn't clamber off Jesse's lap fast enough. Madder than a bull seeing red, she marched toward the dance hall, only to have a strong hand close around her wrist and yank her back to the side of the car.

"You go on ahead, Willie," Jesse said as he backed her up against the car door. His tone was deceptively calm, but the way he held her warned her that there was nothing calm about how he was feeling. "We'll catch up in a minute."

A moment of tense silence passed before Amanda heard Willie's footsteps crunch on the gravel of the parking lot. She listened in seething rage as the sound faded, then blended with the boom of a bass guitar drifting out of the open windows of the saloon.

The early summer night was cool and still. Amanda was vaguely aware of the faint breeze on her heated face as they stood there, him holding her gaze with his own, her holding her tongue because she had no idea what would come out of her mouth if she opened it.

"Do you want to tell me what this is all about?" he asked in a steely voice.

Hovering somewhere between wishing he would drag her into his arms and kiss her, and wanting to knock his thick block off his too-broad shoulders, Amanda feigned interest in the first sprinkling of stars on the horizon. "I don't know what you're talking about."

"I'm talking about the complete turn around you've

executed in the past few hours," he said, anger edging into his tone. "This morning you'd have eaten dirt before you'd let me touch you. Now tonight, out of the blue, you couldn't settle that cute little butt of yours deep enough into my lap—"

"Now wait a minute—"

"And you couldn't press those soft, sweet breasts against my chest often enough. No!" he said, when she opened her mouth again. Grasping her shoulders, he gave her a shake and made her look up at him. "You've been accusing me of playing games since that first night I found you peeking around the lilacs. Tell me, who's playing games now, Sunshine?"

There was fire in his blue eyes, smoke in every breath that fanned her face. "You're baiting me, Amanda, and so help me, if it keeps up, you're going to find yourself caught in your own trap."

Embarrassed by his accurate conclusion of actions she'd thought were subtle and seductive, Amanda closed her eyes. "I—I thought . . ." she began hesitantly, only to be cut off by his low growl.

"The hell you did! You didn't think at all. You're going to think about this, though. I have been up-front with you from day one. You've known what I want. You've known how I feel. But I won't put up with your silliness any longer. For too damn long I've listened to you deny that you want me when you turned hot and panting beneath my hands. For too long I've put up with your viper's tongue and cold shoulder while your eyes said take me to bed."

As if suddenly realizing that he held her shoulders in a bone-crushing grip, Jesse slowly lifted his hands away. "A man has limits, Amanda. Tonight, you've pushed me to mine." He drew a deep, steadying breath and locked his gaze on hers. "So don't you come dancing around me like a mare in season, just to tease then not deliver. I won't be used that way. I want you, yes. But I want it all, Amanda. Not just the flirting. Not just the sex. All of it. But I'm getting damn tired of watching you reduce what's happening between us to a game, where you decide to change the rules every time you feel a little threatened. You're a woman. When you decide to act like one, you know where to find me."

The Lady Slipper was the oldest and most popular of the town's limited night spots. Built by an insightful businessman who recognized the allure of Montana's Old West heritage, the Slipper's Wild West saloon motif had stood the dance hall and bar in good stead with both the local patrons and the tourists for nearly fifty years. Some of her customers had aged right along with her. Willie Brady was one of them.

A very subdued Amanda spotted him among the boisterous crowd as she pushed through the swinging doors. She made her way through the legions of partying cowboys and cowgirls to join him, perching herself on the only empty stool left at the long, polished bar.

"You look like you could use a beer," Willie said above the music and rowdy chatter.

"What I need is to have my head examined. I'll settle for the beer, though." She forced a smile for Willie's benefit, then looked over her shoulder into the crowd.

Amanda felt like a fool, and rightfully so. Once again, she'd proven that where Jesse Kincannon was concerned, she couldn't seem to help herself. He was right on every count. First, she'd denied her attraction to him. Then she'd stupidly declared all-out war. Now, when she was ready to admit defeat and fall headlong into his arms, she couldn't even execute a pass sophisticated enough to convince him she was ready for a relationship. He was out of her league, pure and simple.

And he'd read her like a book. It was humiliating. Then again, maybe it was a good thing, she decided, knocking back a deep swallow of her beer. He was dangerous. If she *had* allowed herself the pleasure of an affair with Jesse, she would just have been hurt when he got bored with the situation and left. The more she thought about it, the more she realized she wasn't ready to be hurt that badly. She'd survived Todd, but she hadn't really loved him. This time, she might not be able to recover.

"Pretty quiet tonight, Mandy-girl," Willie commented, watching her face.

She smiled at him and ordered another beer. "Why is it that a nice guy like you never got married, Willie?" she asked, needing a change of subject.

Willie sandwiched his own bottle between his leathery hands and rocked it rhythmically on the bar. "Just weren't in the cards, I guess. No sweet young thing ever looked at me the way I see you look at Jesse."

Amanda groaned. "What? Do I have a sign on my back or something? 'This person is a fool. Make sure you kick her while she's down.'"

"Jesse a little hard on you tonight?"

Amanda snorted.

The gesture made Willie smile. "I'm no dear Adelaide, or Annabelle, or whoever the hell that woman is, but it seems to me that when two people got an itch, it'd be the most natural thing to let each other scratch it."

She shook her head. "You'd think so, wouldn't you? Only it just doesn't seem to be working out that way. Maybe it's not supposed to. It seems like every time . . ." Her voice trailed away as an image in the bar's huge plate glass mirror caught her eye and stole her train of thought.

She swiveled in her seat to get a better look. A better look at Jesse, smiling, tossing back that beautiful head of jet-black hair, and laughing down at the red-haired woman in his arms who wore a coquettish smile, the tightest jeans Amanda had ever seen, and Jesse's dun-colored hat.

Amanda felt the blood drain from her face, felt her palms dampen and her heart rate accelerate to a white-water intensity. Anger, jealousy, humiliation all scrapped inside her for top billing. The man was deliberately trying to drive her crazy. He was succeeding. With a vengeance.

Seeing Amanda grow rigid, Willie spun around to see what had made her so tense. He shoved back his hat with his beer bottle and rested his elbows behind him on the bar as he watched Jesse and the redhead dance by. "Seems like every time what, Amanda?" he prompted as if nothing out of the ordinary had just happened.

"It seems like every time," she began again through clenched teeth, "I come close to satisfying that itch, something brings me to my senses before I make what would undoubtedly be the biggest mistake of my life."

She abruptly whirled around on her stool and ordered another beer.

"For a lightweight, you're hittin' the barley a little heavy and a little fast tonight, aren't ya?"

Amanda laughed at Willie's pretense of casualness. "You know what, Willie? I think you just hit the nail on the head. A lightweight is exactly what I am. And the lightweights of the world are the ones who get knocked around by the heavy hitters like Jesse Kincannon. The key to it all," she stated philosophically, "is finding your weakness and correcting it."

Willie watched with chagrin as she topped off her third beer and ordered another. "Honey, I see the logic in your thinkin', but maybe tonight ain't the night you wanna correct this particular weakness in your character. And do you really think that swillin' down beer like a bull rider trying to find his nerve is the tack you wanna take?"

"I have decided," she said loftily, "that I want to take it any way I can get it." She patted Willie's arm and slipped off the stool. "You have a good time tonight, Willie, and don't you worry about me. I see somebody I want to talk to and by the way he's smiling, I'd say he wants to talk to me too."

Willie scowled as she wound her way across the dance floor to the table where one of their neighboring ranchers Conn Warren and some of his boys were settled in for the night. Conn's Cheshire cat grin lit up the smoky hall like a one-hundred-watt bulb as he stood and made room for Amanda at his table.

Seven

Amanda tried to convince herself she was having a good time with Conn Warren. He was the kind of man she should be interested in. Conn was a straight shooter, a man she could depend on. Hard working. Steady. Reliable. No rascal or rounder here.

When she'd first moved back to the Flying K, Conn had made a bit of a pest of himself. His ranch bordered the Flying K, so it was easy for him to drop in too often and too unexpectedly, then try too hard to get her to go out with him. She'd grown up with him just as she had with Jesse. The three of them had had fun together as kids, and now as a man, Conn was a prize catch by most women's standards. He had a sweet disposition and a charming sense of humor to go along with his all-American good looks. Blonde and brown-eyed like herself, he'd enjoyed pointing out to her how good they would look together and what beautiful babies they could make, not to mention the fun they would have making them.

The problem was, there were never any sparks between her and Conn. The problem was Jesse.

Yet as the evening wore on, she found herself wishing Conn could be the man to stir the fires Jesse had ignited, then purposefully let die. So when Conn suggested they get some air, she went with him. As soon as she stepped outside, she knew it would never happen.

It was a beautiful night. The right sky, the right mood . . . the wrong man.

She leaned back heavily against the building, hoping the cool air would clear her head of thoughts of Jesse.

"I'd about given up on you, Amanda," Conn said amiably as he stood in front of her, resting one hand against the building, above her head. "Somehow I'd gotten the impression you didn't care if you ever saw me again."

She smiled gently, even as she edged away just a bit. His scent, though not unpleasant, was a little overpowering and laced with too much whiskey. "Is that why you stopped dropping by?"

"A man can only field so many cold shoulders before he takes off his glove and goes home."

"Did I give you the cold shoulder?" she asked, feeling truly regretful.

"Colder than January in the mountains," he confirmed with a hangdog look.

"I'm sorry it seemed that way. I didn't mean for you to make yourself so scarce. What I'd really like is for us to be good friends."

He arched an eyebrow. "Friends?"

"Friends, neighbors, like we used to be growing up."

He frowned and moved in closer. Too close. "It could be so much more than that, Amanda."

He lowered his head to hers.

"Conn," she said in surprise, trying to push him away.

"Shhh. Just relax, honey. I've been wanting to get you alone like this for so long. Now don't fight it. It'll be good. You'll see."

There was no stopping him. His mouth was hard and hot, insistent and demanding, as he pinned her between his body and the building, and his hands began a frenzied roaming. She struggled to turn her head away, struggled to free her hands. How could he attack her this way?

"Please! Don't do this," she whispered frantically, when she managed to wrench her mouth away from his.

"You be needin' a little help persuading this critter to back away, Mandy-girl?"

Taken off guard by Willie's unexpected interruption, Conn loosened his hold to look over his shoulder. Amanda seized the moment to wiggle away from his grasp.

"You back off, old man," Conn snarled, his tone suddenly ugly. "This is between the lady and me."

"The lady," Amanda snapped, feeling both anger and humiliation as she tugged the shoulder of her blouse back into place, "has had enough of the *gentleman's* company for one night."

She whirled around and ran smack into the solid wall of Jesse's chest. One look at his face and she knew he'd witnessed the entire, unfortunate incident. Beyond mortification, she slipped around him and headed for the parking lot.

Willie was hot on her trail. "You know the only thing keepin' me from giving you the spankin' you deserve is that you're too old for it."

"Just get me out of here, Willie," she pleaded in a whisper.

"Damn fool kids," Willie muttered as he hailed a group of Flying K hands that was headed back to the ranch.

• • •

Midnight and moonlight spilled through the window of Amanda's bedroom in the foreman's cottage. The night was cool and still, too cool for her to be wearing only her silk kimono, too still to match the thunderous warnings of her heart.

Yet she sat and waited, one bare foot tucked beneath her bottom, the rocker creaking in time to the rhythm of the night.

She'd seen the coldness in Jesse's eyes when he'd found her with Conn outside the Lady Slipper. She'd also seen the disgust. But until she'd come home and let herself think about it, she hadn't realized what else she'd seen. In the depths of his eyes she'd glimpsed a desperate vulnerability. While she'd been busy remembering the sins of the child, she'd forgotten that child's fears. Jesse was still afraid of rejection. Thirty years of pretending to be immune to his father's neglect couldn't conceal the glimmer of fear that had flared in his eyes that night.

Amanda understood now why he'd stayed at the dance and sent her home with Willie, as if he could care less about her. A carefree, flirting Jesse wasn't open to hurt. A caring, needing Jesse was susceptible to pain. How could she ever have thought her vulnerability exceeded his own?

One hour became two, and still she waited, absently stroking the silk belt of her kimono, watching for the headlights to creep up the long, winding drive home.

When at last she heard the rumbling purr of Jesse's Porsche, she moved to the bed. Sitting tensely on its edge, she waited once more . . . but not for long.

Just enough time had passed for Jesse to enter the ranch house and find the blue room empty, when her bedroom door swung open, slamming against the wall with a crack. Jesse filled the door frame, his shoulders broad, his hips narrow. His stance was that of a warrior moving in for an easy kill.

They watched each other in measuring silence, her features illuminated by the sliver of moonlight washing in through the window, his cast in darkness. Instinctively she knew a deep scowl was etched on the angular planes of his face.

"I thought we'd agreed the time for playing games was over," he said at last. His voice held less patience than it did fatigue.

Except for the pounding of blood through her ears, the room was drowned in utter silence. Amanda met his gaze, which cut through the shadows and pinned her where she sat. She clung to the picture of his vulnerability, hoping for the courage to overcome her own. "It is over," she replied.

He watched her for a long, searching moment. "What is this then, Amanda? You knew I wouldn't let you stay here alone. You knew I'd come after you."

She swallowed, then whispered, "I was counting on it."

Faster still, beat her heart. It wasn't fear of Jesse that made her pulse rush so, at least not fear of his anger. It was fear of the wanting, the irrepressible need to end the cat-and-mouse play between them. Fear of the hunger that might never be sated, the love that might never be returned. Fear that in recognizing his need for acceptance, she might lose sight that she needed it too.

The slight relaxing of his shoulders told her he understood what she was offering, and that perhaps, he also understood her fear. Yet he remained in the doorway, and this time, it was he who did the waiting.

"If you're giving me a chance to change my mind,"

she said, sensing the reason for his hesitancy, "I'd appreciate it if you wouldn't be so gallant."

She held out her hand and with it, her heart. "Dance with me, Jesse," she said, telling him she knew the risks. "I didn't get to dance with you tonight."

He strode slowly into the room and stopped in front of her, but didn't touch her. He was so close, she could feel his breath feather across the top of her head, sense the heat and tension in his body. She looked up and met his eyes. The connection was total and sweet. Without a word, he took her hand in his and pulled her to her feet.

Drawing her against him, he simply held her. For a long, silent moment they clung together. Then he began to move. Slowly, seductively, he swayed to a beat that began as his, but ended up as theirs.

Amanda reached up and tugged his Stetson off. Holding it in her hands, she looped her wrists around his neck and nestled her head on his shoulder. He smelled of whiskey and a little of the perfume from the women he'd held in his arms at the dance.

She recalled the redhead wearing his hat and felt a swift pang of jealousy, then pushed it aside. Jesse held her now. Only her. His beautiful hands, hesitant at first, tethered her in a loose embrace before he crushed her against him as if he couldn't pull her close enough. The Stetson hit the floor with a soft thud as she fit herself tightly against him.

The sigh that shuddered through his body was pure release, utter satisfaction. "What took you so long, Sunshine?" he whispered gruffly into her hair.

She swallowed thickly before answering. "I guess I'm just not very good at this, Jess."

His hands drifted down to splay wide on her hips. "At trusting me?"

She heard the edge creep into his voice. "At believing I'm someone you could want."

Cradling her head in his hands, he tipped her face up to his. His eyes held a wealth of wanting. "Then let me make you a believer."

With infinite gentleness, he brushed his lips across her brow, her closed eyes, her cheeks, staking a claim with each whispered kiss, nurturing a hot, licking flame with every worshipful touch of his mouth to her skin. In pieces and bits, he triggered sensual shimmers and throaty sighs, and he taught her the magic of believing.

"Do you have any idea," he asked against her lips as he continued to sway with her to music only he could hear, "how long I've wanted to be with you this way?"

"How long?" she murmured, loving the play of his hands on her body. "What way?"

He smiled against her mouth. "Forever," he replied between deep, silken kisses. "Every way."

"Tell me," she whispered when their open mouths parted. "Show me."

Without breaking the gentle rhythm of their dance, he guided her to the bed. "I think I lost my heart to you when you were all of three and I was seven," he said as he sat down on the edge of the bed and pulled her close to stand between his thighs.

"Way back then?" she asked, smiling lazily as he sandwiched her hips between his hands and nestled her against him.

"Way back then," he said to the warmth between her breasts. He pillowed his head there, as if he loved the feel and the scent of her against his face, the strength of her slender arms looped over his shoulders. "The first time you climbed up on my lap and cuddled against me like a trusting puppy, I swore I'd kill anyone who hurt you."

Amanda grinned. "Tough talk for a toddler. Especially considering that the older you got, the more grief you gave me."

She felt him smile against her breast, then felt the smile fade as his mouth opened to breathe warmth through the thin silk of her kimono to the skin beneath.

His hands skated restlessly up the length of her back before returning to her hips, cupping and caressing her buttocks through the robe. "Sunshine, you don't know grief until you know the torment I went through keeping my hands off you."

"Ah . . . all those runaway hormones."

"Ah . . . all those sweet, fleeting images of you," he countered, suddenly still. He set her a step away from him so he could see her face in the moonlight. "Until one day, the image wasn't so fleeting."

She brushed a lock of hair from his brow. "What are you talking about?"

"Remember how hot July was the last summer I was home from college?"

She nodded slowly, thinking of that summer ten years ago.

"And the little watering hole on the range below the south slope?"

She smiled for a split second before her breath caught. She remembered well the little pool where she used to go skinny-dipping by herself. Dropping her hands to his shoulders, she said a little breathlessly, "I used to ride up there to cool off. Did you go there too?"

"Only once," he said, his voice full of heat as his hands worked the knotted belt at her waist. "But some little blonde had beat me to it. And I didn't cool off. The heat I felt that day has been burning ever since."

"Jesse . . ." she whispered as he untied the sash and placed a sweet, deep kiss on the quivering flesh below her navel.

"I'll never forget how you looked, Sunshine," he

said, pushing her robe more fully open. He spanned her waist with his hands, steadying her as she trembled. "And I've never stopped wanting to see you that way again." Locking his gaze with hers, he let his hands glide up the delicate framework of her ribs. His palms lingered on the soft mounds of her breasts, making her arch and shiver and yearn.

"You were so beautiful, all golden glowing skin, all sleek, elegant muscle." He pushed her robe from one shoulder. "But so young. It was the only thing that kept me from riding down the ridge and taking you then and there."

"I—I thought I was alone," she whispered, watching his face as he touched her.

He chuckled soft and low. "I know. That was part of the fascination. You were completely uninhibited, like a wildcat, nimble and innocent and so damn sexy, I thought I'd die of discomfort before I managed the long ride home."

She moved closer, settling herself intimately between the lee of his thighs. "Serves you right for watching."

"Hell, all I could do was watch . . ." He swallowed thickly, then brushed his lips across her nipple and smiled at her involuntary shiver. "I figured I had at least that much coming to me."

With infinite care, he tugged on the robe, baring her other silky shoulder. The robe snagged on her hands before slipping to the floor like water. His whole body clenched with gut-wrenching wanting as her pale skin was revealed to the moonlight.

"You stood in the middle of that thigh-deep pool," he murmured, "sunshine gilding your skin to gold, glinting off the water droplets that clung to your hair, your skin."

Amanda shuddered at the sensual heat his words created. To think . . . to *know* he'd been watching her. She remembered well the wantonness with which she'd played, gloriously naked and wonderfully free, thinking she was alone.

"I was close enough," he went on, his voice mesmerizing, "to see every shiny, trickling bead as it drizzled over your shoulders." He stood, touching a finger to the curve of her throat. "Down your breasts, between them." His breath was ragged as his hand traced the path the water had taken down her body. "You have the most beautiful breasts, Amanda."

He cupped them in his callused hands, molding her, holding her, inciting her senses to a shattering wanting. He touched her with such intense gentleness, as if he held something as precious as diamonds or gold. He made her feel like a valued treasure as he gathered her against him, then lowered her onto the bed.

"I was jealous of water. Water," he repeated as if even he couldn't believe it. "I didn't want anything against you but me. I wanted it to be my mouth caressing you, my tongue touching you."

Aching for his words to become reality, she pressed trembling fingers to his cheek. "Touch me now, Jess," she begged in breathless anticipation as he leaned over her. "Touch me now . . ."

At the first tentative caress of his mouth on her skin, she cried out. Molten heat spiraled in a long, sensual burn from the tip of her breast to the center of her femininity, where it coiled to a pulsing ache. Jesse wrapped her tightly against him, his mouth hot and greedy, his kisses thorough and slow. He tasted her from breast to belly and back again with a languor that drove her to the brink of insanity.

"Jesse!" she cried as he drew deeply on her breast. He let go, but only to move to her other breast and seduce and suckle and soothe her back to aching awareness of her need for him.

When he lifted himself off her, she shivered in protest. But when he returned, ah, when he returned, he was as gloriously naked as she was, his skin as blisteringly hot as her own. Where his mouth had laid trails of wanting, his body now promised fulfillment.

"Sweet, sweet Amanda," he murmured before claiming her mouth in a long, searing kiss. His tongue took liberties that she invited, swirling deep into her mouth, dancing with her own tongue as they had danced in the moonlight in her bedroom. With exquisite tenderness, he cupped the feminine curls at the juncture of her thighs. The lean fingers that coaxed such beautiful music from his battered old guitar, now played her body to lush readiness.

When he broke the kiss, they were both breathing heavily. Perspiration beaded Jesse's brow. Amanda moved sinuously beneath him, restless to have him a part of her.

"I want you, Sunshine. Trust me enough. Believe me enough to let this happen."

In answer, she trailed her hands down his back to stroke and boldly cup his hips to hers.

He groaned, nudging her legs apart and settling his heat between them. "Say you want this as much as I do."

"I want this, Jess. I want you. Please, please come inside me. I've wanted you there for so long."

"How long?" he rasped against her ear as he fit himself to her body.

"Forever . . ." she whispered on a low, silken sigh.

"What way?" he demanded, filling her.

"Every way," she answered when she could form the words. "Every way . . . Jesse . . ." And she cried his name as he drove deep within her.

He was all hot, glowing need, all steamy, masculine strength, as he murmured love words and lust words and begged her to go with him. "Show me," he commanded with gentle urgency. "Tell me."

Placing her fate completely in his hands, she wrapped her legs around his hips and whispered her need for him. With total trust and delicious abandon, she let him tumble her over the edge of reality into a realm of sensation she'd only dreamed existed.

Amanda roused herself what seemed like a glorious lifetime later. With slumberous wonder, she watched the man asleep in her bed. His loving had held such tenderness and such urgency. She knew better than to believe he loved her. Oh, he cared. But this was Jesse. Jesse who loved women, who talked of wanting, of possession. Last night it was she he'd needed. And she'd given in to his need, because there *was* love here. Her love. It would have to be enough.

It wasn't enough, she admitted bleakly as she lay in his arms, falling back asleep as she listened to the rhythm of his deep, even breathing. It would never be enough.

Jesse's lazy caresses woke her hours later. She gave herself to him again with wonder and awe, experiencing a growing sense of freedom that was totally at odds with his complete possession of her body and her spirit.

She ignored the niggling feeling that she should be frightened of the way she was tumbling headlong into this relationship with him. When he emerged from her shower at first light wearing nothing but that renegade grin and a damp towel, she shoved her fears aside and plunged in headfirst.

Except for Jesse's Stetson, which she'd plopped at a rakish angle over her tangled hair, she sat as naked as the day she was born in the middle of her thoroughly mussed-up bed.

"Hey, cowboy," she said with a saucy grin. "Wanna get lucky?"

With a husky chuckle and a wicked glint in his devil blue eyes, he whipped the towel from his hips and dove for the bed. Amid shrieks of laughter and feigned capitulation, he let her wrestle him to his back. When the jostling was over, she was sitting astride his lap. Judging by the look on his face, it was exactly where he wanted her.

Snagging his hat from the sheets where it had fallen in the tussle, he placed it back on her head, then lowered his hands to her hips. She felt the flush of excitement brighten her cheeks as he gazed at her naked breasts, swollen and pink from last night's loving.

His smile faded. "You are beautiful." His eyes half-closed as his hot gaze caressed her. "Hang on, little cowgirl," he murmured in a deep, sensual rasp as he lifted her, then eased her down over his heat. "Let Jesse take you for a ride."

She gasped as he embedded himself deep within her. Lord, how she loved him, loved the power of him, the fullness, the way he fit inside her. Love and fear became one in a blinding moment of need. "Promise me one thing, Jess . . ." she heard herself beg in a desperate whisper.

"Anything," he growled, clenching his jaw against her slow, sinuous motion above him.

"For as long as your boots are under my bed, no other cowgirl wears this hat."

Her answer was a low, delicious moan as Jesse rode with her to the rhythm as old as time, to an end as explosive as thunder.

• • •

"Tina tells me you got a call from your folks," Jesse said casually.

He and Amanda were riding the north range, running a tally of the calf count, making decisions about whether to move this segment of the herd this week, or whether the grass would hold out until the end of the month.

Amanda pulled Eclipse to a stop and nodded, thinking with wonder how easy it was to love Jesse. It had been a week since they'd become lovers. Since they'd become friends. They'd long since moved her things out of the cottage and into his master bedroom in the ranch house.

"Daddy was just checking up on me," she said. "Making sure I eat my Wheaties, tighten my cinch strap, that sort of thing."

Jesse reined in beside her. Crossing his forearms on the pommel, he studied her face as he asked, "And how does Daddy feel about his little girl taking up with the riffraff?"

She smiled guiltily. "The subject didn't come up."

"No?" His mouth tightened. "Just when were you planning on telling them?"

She looked away, unable to face his hurt, and not wanting him to see her own. Tell them what? she asked silently. Tell them I love you? Tell them you love me? How could she tell them something she didn't know? Jesse had never said he loved her. He'd never hinted at where this was leading, or if he would even stay. She hedged. "When the time is right."

He said nothing. He just sat there with that little-boy look on his face that she seldom saw but never failed to melt her heart.

"Would you like to know," she asked, caught between twin urges to see that look a little longer and to put a smile back on his face, "when I decided you weren't the outlaw I always figured you to be?

"It was that Sunday a couple of weeks ago," she went on when he didn't answer. "The day I found you and the boys behind the barn playing basketball."

She smiled at the memory. "In the first place, I couldn't believe you could coax that crew into getting off their duffs on their day off. But to actually see them shirtless, in their ten-gallons, jeans, and boots stumbling around that makeshift court like a tumbleweed edition of the Globetrotters . . ." She paused, then turned her grin on him. "Well, let's just say, I realized that day what a special kind of man you are."

Although he was quiet the rest of the afternoon, Amanda knew all was forgiven when he met her at the bedroom door that night in his boots and his britches, a basketball tucked in the crook of his arm. "How 'bout a little one-on-one?" he drawled as he led her, grinning, to the bed.

Eight

This is paradise, Amanda thought that night as she fell asleep in Jesse's arms. But everyone knew paradise wasn't real, that it never lasted. She wanted her paradise to be the exception. The next day, she faced the fact that it wasn't.

The beginning of the end started when Lucy paid an unannounced visit to the Flying K the next morning. It was paperwork day, the day Amanda dreaded each month. But with a mug of coffee to fortify her and a month's worth of bookkeeping to catch up on, she resolutely shut herself in the den in the ranch house and dug in. After balancing the ledgers—and fighting off the depression caused by the depleted state of the checkbook—she was about to attack a week's worth of unopened mail when the door to the study opened.

Expecting Jesse or Willie, she was totally unprepared when Jesse's sister, Lucy, walked into the room.

"You needn't look so surprised, Amanda," Lucy said with an insincere smile. "You had to have known

I'd show up sometime, if for no other reason than to see if the place was crumbling around your feet."

Ignoring the slur, Amanda closed the account books and folded her hands on top of them. "If you came to see Jesse, I suspect you'll find him working on the barn."

A frown furrowed Lucy's high forehead. "I heard about that fire," she said a bit distantly. "Unfortunate."

"Yes," Amanda agreed, wondering where this was leading. "It was unfortunate."

She waited in edgy silence as Lucy slowly wandered around what used to be her father's den. Amanda couldn't help but note the resemblance between Lucy and Jesse. The differences, however, were more pronounced. Where Jesse was always quick with a smile or a tease, Lucy was sober to the point of stoic. The years had sharpened her already-angular features instead of mellowed them, and her own bitterness had done the rest of the damage. She could have been a beautiful woman, but her perpetual frown had turned her, instead, into a shrew.

"We want to sell," Lucy said abruptly, not bothering to look up from the book she'd slipped off a shelf. "Jesse and I want to sell."

"Jesse hasn't said anything about selling."

Lucy calmly replaced the book and turned to Amanda, her smile condescending. "Of course not, dear. He's been too busy seducing you. Ah." She laughed. "I see by your stricken expression that I'm right. Well, that was the plan of course, to wait until he could coerce you into seeing things our way, but frankly, we're running out of time."

Amanda could only stare at her in stunned silence.

"Oh, for heaven's sake," Lucy exclaimed, "grow up and look at things realistically, will you? Do you really think that Jesse would settle for a life on this ranch after where he's been, what he's done? Do you honestly think he'd settle for you?" She shook her head impatiently. "Either way you slice it, Amanda, you lose. You can stay with him and be humiliated when he leaves you, or you can hang on here a few months longer until your money runs out and you're forced to cry uncle, or—and pay attention now, because this is the good part—you can cash in now, tell yourself you had a little adventure, and leave with some money in your pocket."

Drawing what strength she had left around her, Amanda rose, walked to the door, and opened it. "Get out."

Lucy stopped squarely in front of her. "Oh, dear. I can see we've got our feelings hurt. Frankly, I don't give a damn about your feelings. You're as much of a tramp as your mother was, and I want you out of here. I want you to agree to the sale of this property. But just to show you I'm a good sport, if you're quick about it, I'll even put in a good word for you with Jesse. Maybe he'll stick around and service you a while longer."

It was an hour before Amanda quit shaking. And when the shaking stopped, the nausea set in. Lucy was a cruel, vicious woman. And damn her, she'd voiced every one of Amanda's fears about Jesse. She wouldn't believe her. She wouldn't. Jesse didn't care about selling the ranch. He'd told her so repeatedly. Jesse cared about her.

Determined not to let Lucy's attack get to her, Amanda launched her own assault on the stack of morning mail. It wasn't until she'd gotten into the body of the first letter from a company whose letterhead boasted "International Growth," that she realized this particular piece was meant for Jesse.

Though she knew she should fold it up and lay it aside for him, she couldn't make herself put it down after she'd read the first sentence. The shaking started again.

> *I just wanted to follow up our phone conversation of last week with a letter to restate our position and thank you again for your willingness to consider our proposal. We are more than willing to negotiate further on the final figure for the Flying K. I am sure we can come to an amiable settlement that will benefit both you, your sister, and Ms. Carter.*

Amanda's heart thundered as she forced herself to hold the expensive stationery still. Feeling betrayed and frighteningly aware that she was about to lose what she held most dear, she read on.

> *While I understand your desire to postpone the sale until all parties are willing to sell, I must caution you that too long a delay may jeopardize the terms of the contract and deter the company's major investors toward, if you'll pardon the metaphor, greener pastures. At this point in time, they are still willing to wait for your final go-ahead. I cannot guarantee, however, that next month they will be as agreeable.*
>
> *Every day more ranch owners are cashing in on the current boom in land prices. While the Flying K would make an excellent prospect for subdivisions, other properties of equal import may become available prior to your decision and subsequently, the price we may be able to offer in the future may be reflective of availability of other land.*

*It would be in everyone's best interests if
you could persuade Ms. Carter as soon as
possible. With those issues in mind, we will
leave it up to you to reopen dialogue concerning the sale. Please don't wait too long,
Mr. Kincannon, or the bandwagon may be
full.*

Stunned, heart-bruised Amanda reread the letter,
searching for a glimmer of evidence that Jesse was
not a willing participant. She found none. Everything verified that Lucy had been telling the truth.

She looked up when she heard the door creak open
and saw Jesse walking into the den. She wanted to
run from the whole sordid mess. A measure of how
far gone she was, was that it was his arms she
wanted to run to. She fought the wanting and clung
desperately to what dignity she had left.

"I'd ask how it's going," he said, "but judging from
the look on your face, I think I already know the
answer." He smiled sympathetically and slapped the
dust from the thighs of his jeans, then settled into
the blood-red leather chair that sat at a right angle to
the desk. It wasn't until he'd leaned back and truly
looked at her that he realized more than book work
was bothering her.

"Amanda?"

She rose stiffly, buffeting herself against the pain.
"Your sister paid me a little visit today."

"Lucy was here?"

Amanda nodded but couldn't look at him.

"What did she have to say?"

She laughed tightly. "Plenty. She had plenty to say."

"I take it she was her own sweet self where you're
concerned."

"Sweet as battery acid."

"Baby, I'm sorry."

She looked at him sharply. After a moment's hesitation she held out the letter. "I opened this by mistake," she said in a controlled voice.

Hugging her arms around her waist, she turned to face the window behind the desk. "I seem to be making a lot of mistakes lately, some of which your sister was kind enough to point out."

The room was funeral quiet as she waited for his response. She wanted to hear his explanation, wanted, heaven help her, to hear even his lies if they could make this hurt go away.

She sensed his tension as he rose from the chair and circled the desk until he stood directly behind her.

"I thought we'd come to terms, you and I," he said quietly.

"The only terms that seem to be of importance are those surrounding the sale of the ranch." She faced him, her eyes filled with angry tears. "I won't sell, Jesse. No matter how persuasive you've managed to be. I may be a fool, but I'm a stubborn one. And I learned my lessons well."

"I thought you did," he said, shaking his head. "I thought you had learned to trust me."

"I *did* trust you," she snapped.

"I didn't invite this letter, Amanda. I didn't initiate it, I didn't encourage it."

"Thank you for your willingness to consider our proposal," she paraphrased acidly. "We are willing to negotiate and to wait for you to convince Ms. Carter of her desire to sell." Her tone dared him to deny the truth in those words. "Well, nice try, cowboy. I'll give you credit. You are convincing as hell. Not once did you mention selling out when we were between the sheets. Not once did you make me think you wanted what we had together for anything other than myself.

When were you going to pop the big question? Somewhere between 'you wanna get naked?' and—"

"Stop it!" Jesse cut her off, grabbing her by her upper arms and hauling her against him.

She wrenched herself away with a strength that surprised them both. "No! You stop it! Stop lying. Stop your sweet-talking. Stop this farce of caring!" She was crying now. She couldn't help it and she hated herself for her weakness. "Dammit, Jesse, you owe me! You owe me at least the decency of being honest with me."

He stared at her, his stance growing rigid. "She really did a number on you, didn't she?"

"She merely let the third partner in on the entire plan. More than decent of her I'd say."

"There is no plan, Amanda. There's just you and me. And that damn frail ego of yours that won't let you believe I love you."

Her hand flew to her mouth to trap an hysterical laugh. "You love me? Oh. Oh, that's rich! You're really pulling out the big guns now, aren't you?"

His eyes grew darker, his stance more controlled, as she felt herself fall apart in front of him.

"I'll do whatever it takes to convince you that what I care about is you," he said. "Look, I don't know what Lucy told you, but I can tell you what I told her. The last time I saw her, which was about a week ago, she begged me to convince you to sell. I told her you weren't interested and as far as I was concerned, that meant the subject was closed."

Damning him for lying, damning herself for halfway believing him, Amanda asked, "How do you explain this letter?"

"Amanda, those people are hard sell. They called me, yes. I'd guess it was at Lucy's urging. But I did not encourage them. What you read is their interpretation of our conversation, not mine. You don't want to sell. We don't sell. End of discussion."

She stared at him, unable to hide her confusion and her longing to believe him.

"Amanda." He spoke her name with an edge of frustrated anger. She turned away from him to gaze again out the window. He sighed heavily. "I thought my fight was over. I thought I'd finally convinced you to trust me. I need that from you, Amanda. As much as I need your love."

The hurt, the ever so carefully veiled plea in his statement, reached out to her. She turned, raising tear-filled eyes to his. "I want to. I want to trust you."

"Do I make it so hard?"

She pinched her eyes shut and bit on her lower lip to quell the trembling. She thought of the past days and nights of his loving. Of the things he'd said. Of the things he'd done. In the end, it was his actions, not Lucy's cruel words, she chose to believe. Her pride intervened too. It simply hurt too much not to trust him. "Help me, Jesse," she whispered, giving in at last. "Hold me."

He crushed her in his arms before she could complete the words. "Always, Sunshine. I'll always hold on to you. I love you. Believe that. Hold on to it."

Every day during the next week, Amanda marveled at the ways Jesse found to make her a believer. With subtle statements, selfless loving, total and free rein over the running of the ranch, he led her through the maze of her muddled emotions until she surrendered her defenses completely.

The proof of her uncategorical trust surprised even Amanda as she peeked out the window of the den one morning, trying for at least the tenth time to catch another glimpse of him. Willie and the men were gone. They were finishing up the spring calf count she and Jesse had started in preparation for the roundup next week. Jesse had stayed behind. Evidently, it was his morning to "watch" her. She smiled at his protectiveness. Only two weeks ago, she would have snarled.

Under the pretense of catching up on the mail she'd started then neglected the other day, she'd covertly watched Jesse on and off all morning. From her desk in the den, she could see straight to the paddocks and the barn where he was working alone. She loved to watch him. He moved with fluid, purposeful grace as he put the finishing touches on the reconstruction work at the south end of the barn.

It was now midmorning and it was getting warm. Evidently too warm for Jesse, for he'd stripped down to his jeans. Amanda held back the curtain with a trembling hand, a different kind of heat flowing through her as she watched him. A liquid, yearning heat that a woman can only feel for her man.

His shoulders and chest wore a satin sheen of sweat. Clinging to his temples and nape, his too-long hair was spiked and curled with moisture. Steeped in the memories of their lovemaking, she could almost feel the texture of his skin. Almost taste it, almost touch the heavy, silken tangle of his hair.

He was utterly, irrevocably male. An outlaw. And he'd convinced her he loved her. At least for today. Tomorrow he might leave her. She knew it, yet she couldn't control her love for him. Couldn't stay away from him. She was as drawn by the magic that was Jesse Kincannon, as the tides were drawn by the moon.

He'd cast a spell over her. It had to be a spell. An unpossessed Amanda Carter would never even contemplate what she was about to do.

Feeling helplessly, wantonly female, she hurried to her bedroom to change clothes.

It was dark inside the barn. The only light came from the sunshine that snuck down through the high dormers, filtering to pale, hazy cylinders for dust fragments to dance through on their path to the sawdust-covered floor.

"Jesse?" she called softly as she walked toward Eclipse's new stall. The sedate cotton blouse she'd pulled on felt abrasive to her sensitive nipples as the fabric grazed over her bare skin. With every measured step, the denim of the skirt she'd worn dancing sensitized the already-tingling flesh of her thighs.

"Jesse?" she repeated, and wondered at the wild beating of her heart, at the blood-warming anticipation that hummed through her body like a sultry south wind, stirring her yearnings, stoking her longings for Jesse.

Jesse. She sensed him behind her before she felt his breath on her shoulder, before she absorbed his heat at her back.

"Don't you know," he whispered gruffly into her hair, "you can get into big trouble sneaking up on a man like that?"

She leaned back against him, covering the broad, tanned hands that caressed her belly with her own. "I've been in trouble since the day you came back."

His chuckle was wicked and wise and very, very smug. "Sunshine, if you keep talking to me in that low, husky purr, I'm going to have to introduce you to more trouble than you've ever known before."

Her breath caught as his hands began their artful seduction of her body. With one he held her tightly around her waist; with the other he cupped and kneaded her breast. "What's this?" he murmured

when he encountered nothing but warm flesh beneath the demure cotton. "Oh, sweet girl." He nuzzled her arched neck, kissing the tender skin
beneath her ear. "I think maybe I'm the one in
trouble here."

It was her turn to laugh, until his other hand slid
down the length of her leg before tunneling under her
skirt. With a slow, deliberately tantalizing glide, he
skimmed his callused fingers up her inner thigh.
"Amanda," he groaned when he encountered not the
cotton of her underwear, but the satin skin of her
hip, the silken curls of her femininity. "Amanda,
honey . . . you don't have on any panties."

Laughing at the wonder in his discovery, she spun
away, taking advantage of his stunned reaction. Eyes
shining with the confidence of a woman's power, her
skin flushed with the heat of her own shocking
behavior, she backed away a step. "You told me to get
rid of them, remember? So I did. I'm on my way into
town to shop for something more . . . to your lik-
ing. I just stopped by to let you know where I was
going. And to make sure you thought about me while
I was gone."

"You aren't going anywhere," he said, his eyes
looking dark and dangerous.

She smiled uncertainly as he advanced toward her.
She had wanted to surprise him, to tantalize him,
the way he tantalized her. To build the anticipation.
But she was new at this teasing game and she'd had
no conception of her power. "Jesse?"

"Get over here." His voice was deep and unsteady,
and the look in his eyes left no room for interpretation. She felt the full force of her power then, and
with it a shiver of fear. Not that he'd hurt her. It was
fear of her own reaction. She had thought she could
tease, incite, then walk away with complete control.

She was wrong. It was Jesse, always Jesse, who had control.

"Amanda . . ."

As excited now as he was, she shook her head slowly, a token gesture of resistance.

"Oh, yes. Oh. Yes." He grabbed her arm and dragged her with him to Eclipse's stall.

"Jess," she whispered breathlessly as he backed her up to the solid new wall and made fast work of the buttons on her blouse.

"Jess . . . what if—Oh, Lord, Jesse . . ." She trembled as he jerked the demure cotton down her shoulder and bared her breast. "Jess, what if Willie—"

"Willie isn't within four miles of this barn," he growled. His breath hot, his tongue wet, he closed his mouth over her exposed nipple.

"Jess . . . Jess." She groaned and knotted her hands in his hair, forcing his head up to hers. "I don't think—"

"Don't think!" he demanded, and crushed his mouth over hers, pinning her against the stall with his body.

The scent of new wood, fresh hay, and aroused male rushed across her senses like a dark, midnight dream. A dream of Jesse, her reckless lover, with the devil eyes and the wicked, insatiable mouth.

Fingers threaded in his hair, her body arched to his, she met his rapacious, probing kisses with the hunger of a woman in love. As much the conqueror as the conquered, as much the victor as the vanquished, she surrendered willingly to the sweetest defeat she'd ever known.

She felt deliciously out of control and decidedly wanton as he reached between their bodies and tugged her skirt above her waist. He held her gaze with his hot, branding look of possession as he lifted her high against him and guided her legs around his waist.

Gasping as her bare skin met the buckle of his belt, the coarse denim of his jeans, she molded her body to his, giving herself completely to his magic.

"Understand this, Amanda . . ." His eyes grew dark with intent, his voice gruff with passion and purpose as he unbuckled his belt. "You are mine. Now. Always. I have waited for you for what seems like my entire life and I'll never let you go. Never."

She cried his name as he entered her with a swift, explosive thrust. Knotting his hands in her hair, he pressed his lips to her throat, scraping his teeth against her fragrant skin as he kissed his way to her mouth. "Say it, Amanda."

She heard passion, pleading, and unbending determination in his voice as he rocked his body against hers, making her his with each powerful stroke, demanding her surrender with each shuddering breath. "Say it!" he insisted again, urgently.

"I love you, Jess," she cried, knowing she meant it with every breath that was in her. "I love you."

With a ragged groan, he buried himself deep inside her. Covering her mouth with his own, he swallowed her profession of love as she breathlessly repeated her litany against his mouth.

"Kitty, Kitty?" Willie called. "What big ol' fat bird did you swallow for breakfast to put a smile like that on your face?"

Amanda reined in with a start, snapping her gaze to her foreman. She was supposed to be helping him sort cattle. Instead, she'd been remembering the day before when Jesse had made love to her in the barn. Blushing deep scarlet at the memory, she said, "I'm sorry, what did you say?"

"I said," Willie began as he shifted his hips in the saddle, "it sure is a nice day."

"The best," she agreed, oblivious to his tolerant grin. "If the weather holds, we should make short work of moving these beauties to the summer pasture."

"If the weather holds, and the creeks don't run dry, every rancher in the valley will be rolling in George Washington green. And if the markets don't drop, and if you don't have no more 'accidents' . . ." His voice trailed off pointedly.

"Okay, I get the message. *If* it weren't for a hundred variables that could plague every ranch from here to the coast, there would never be a need to worry about cutting a tidy profit, would there? And every rancher in the valley could live happily ever after."

"Just don't want you burying your head in the sand, Mandy-girl. You're not out of the woods yet. Lots of grief can happen before you get those beeves to market in the fall."

She looked out over the stock and across the lush green valley. "Is that what I'm doing, Willie? Am I burying my head in the sand and seeing only what I want to see?"

When she turned to him, Willie diverted his gaze across the valley as she had. "We still talkin' about cattle?"

She dropped her head down, then drew a weary breath. "I don't know, are we?"

"You went and fell in love with him, didn't you?"

"Have I made a big mistake, Willie?" she asked, hating herself for her wavering faith in Jesse.

"He makes you happy, don't he?"

She nodded. "But for how long? He says he loves me. I think he does. But I don't hear anything about tomorrow from him. I don't even know if he's capable of a commitment. Willie, what kind of man can walk away from his home, then ten years later return and not even show any concern about going back to his job. I don't even know if he has a job, how he supports himself."

"I thought he wrote songs or somethin'."

"Or something," she echoed, disgusted with herself. "Listen to me. I've got no right to impose my standards on Jesse, or to measure him against them."

"But you got a right to your curiosity, and if this is as serious as it sounds, you got a right to some answers."

"Maybe I don't really want to know the answers."

"And maybe you just don't know the right questions."

Eclipse swished his tail at a horsefly and fidgeted beneath her. "Maybe I don't at that," she said, nudging the stallion with her knees. "And maybe I'm looking for trouble where there is none."

"Time'll do the tellin'," Willie said, urging his mount into step beside her. "Just give it a little time."

But when Amanda rode back into the paddock late that afternoon, she discovered her time had run out. Jesse was gone, leaving only a hastily scribbled note that was dismally lacking in details.

Sunshine, he'd written, *I hate it more than you do that I have to leave without saying good-bye. Something came up that needs my attention in Tennessee. Miss me. Love me. Trust me. I'll be back as soon as I can. Jess.*

For five empty, agonizing days she ached from the sting of his sudden departure, but clung to his promise to return. He filled her thoughts waking and sleeping—until disaster struck again.

Nine

Once again, they'd picked fire.

Amanda suppressed a violent shudder brought on by fear, fatigue, and the sudden cooling of the evening air. Leaning heavily against a truck, she surveyed the damage. A charred black sea of broken dreams and swirls of smoke lay before her in mocking silence. The blaze had started sometime after midnight and had finally burned itself out at dusk. But not before it had swept across hundreds of acres of hay ground, consuming over half of her winter feed for the stock cows.

"I'm sorry, Amanda."

She looked up at Fire Marshal Rawlings. "You're doing all you can, I know."

"One of these times, this bastard's going to make a mistake. And when he does, we'll nail him."

She nodded, but felt no real conviction. Only defeat.

"You gonna be all right, honey?" Rawlings asked.

"Sure. You go on home now. Martha's got to be wondering if you're okay."

Rawlings gave her shoulder a squeeze, then shaking his head, he walked toward his truck.

Amanda watched with a weary heart as Willie separated himself from the hands who were still working the edge of the firebreak. He looked so old as he walked toward her, so tired. She felt tears gather. He didn't deserve this any more than she did. He loved the Flying K. It was his home. She hated the look of frustration, the helplessness she saw in his watery eyes.

Damn you, Jesse, she cursed silently. *Why aren't you here? Willie needs you. I need you.*

She climbed into the passenger side of the truck as Willie approached. He didn't say a word, but just slid in behind the wheel and cranked on the ignition.

His silence summed it up. There was nothing left to say that hadn't been said before. The fire wasn't the beginning, but only the latest in a string of disasters since Jesse had left. More fences down. More cattle lost. More tainted water in the big reservoir. After nearly a month's hiatus, it was happening all over again. Only this time, Amanda wasn't sure she could survive the setbacks.

Whoever was doing this wanted the Flying K out of business. Lucy wanted to sell, but despite the woman's determination, her bitterness, Amanda couldn't make herself believe Lucy was responsible. So, there remained a vast, glaring question. Who? And to what end? She caught a glimpse of Jake Slater shuffling around in the shadows. She couldn't believe he was the answer either. He had no motive. It made no sense.

Willie drove the truck in a wide circle and headed for the main house. Leaning her head wearily against the back of the seat, Amanda gave in to the fatigue as one question after another plagued her. One in particular distanced all the others. Where was Jesse?

• • •

The next afternoon Amanda was standing near the stockyard fence, discussing her latest dilemma with a grim-faced Willie, when Conn Warren arrived in his pickup.

Willie, overplaying the role of protector in Jesse's absence, snagged his toothpick out of his mouth and pushed himself away from the fence. "You want me and the boys to invite him to leave?" he asked Amanda, just loud enough for Conn to hear.

"Relax," Conn said with a good-natured grin. "I come in peace."

Willie held his ground. Conn shot Amanda a comically pleading look.

She ignored his bid for sympathy. "What can we do for you, Conn?"

He glanced from Amanda to Willie, then shook his head in a show of self-deprecation. "I've played the fool a few times in my life, Amanda, but never more than the night at the Lady Slipper. I'd like to blame the whiskey and a little of my own frustration, but that would be the coward's way out. The truth is, I was a flat-out bastard and I'm sorry as hell. Do you think you can find it in your heart to forgive me?"

"She can't," Willie said flatly. "Now, git."

Amanda was just exhausted enough to be tickled by Willie's abrupt dismissal and Conn's shocked expression.

"Willie," she said, gentling her laughter with affection, "I think Conn came with good intentions."

Willie snorted.

Conn threw Amanda a grateful grin, then addressed Willie. Apparently he recognized that if he was going to break this particular barrier, he was going to have to get through Willie first. "I was wrong, and I'm here to make up for it. I hear you've been having a little trouble." He looked directly at Amanda. "I figured you could use some neighborly help."

Willie scratched his chin, still looking like he'd just as soon bulldog Warren and brand him as a louse. "It's your call, Mandy-girl," he said finally.

"I say forgive and forget." To reinforce her decision, she smiled at Conn. "Come on, I'm dry. Let's all go up to the house. Tina's in town getting supplies, but if you'll give me a chance to rinse the dust off my face, I'll find us something cool to drink."

"I'll just head on down to the barn to check on that mare that got a hold of that bad water," Willie said. "I'm a holler away if you need me," he added for Amanda's benefit, though he stared straight at Conn when he said it.

Conn held up his hands. "Hey, you don't have to worry about her, okay?"

Willie snorted doubtfully, but he turned and ambled to the barn in his bowlegged, arthritic gait.

"The old boy's age is starting to show on him," Conn remarked as he followed Amanda across the back porch and into the cool kitchen.

"I worry about him sometimes," she said. "Especially now when he has so much to do." Not caring about decorum, she bent over the sink, filled her cupped palms with water from the tap, and rinsed the dust from her face and neck. "Oh, that felt good," she murmured into a hand towel as she dried off. "Now, about that drink I promised you." She searched the interior of the refrigerator. "Is a beer okay?"

"Whatever you're having."

"I'm having iced tea."

"Sounds fine."

Setting a glass in front of each of them, Amanda took a seat opposite Conn at the table.

"Been a long time since I sat in this kitchen," he

said, looking everywhere but at her. "Hasn't changed much."

"Everything's changed," she said heavily.

"Yeah, I guess it has." He ran his thumb along the frosting of sweat on his glass. "Amanda—"

"Conn—"

They both spoke at once, then stopped just as abruptly.

The uncomfortable tension humming between them was not going to be resolved, Amanda thought, until they dealt honestly with the night at the Lady Slipper.

Conn rubbed the back of his neck and swore softly. "Damn but I hate this." He slanted her a thoughtful look. "You remember the day old man Meyers caught me throwing spitballs in his eighth grade biology class?"

She smiled. "Instead of kicking you out on your ear, he made you get up in front of the class and read aloud the chapter on reproduction of the human species."

"I'd never felt like a bigger fool . . . until now."

"I can see that you do," she said wryly and with relief.

"Can we forget it ever happened?"

"Consider it forgotten. I've got enough to worry about without nursing a grudge against an old friend."

He sighed with relief. "Thank you for that. Since we're being so painfully honest here, there's something else I need for you to know. Sorry as I am for the way I handled it, I'm not sorry about the kiss. I still feel the same way about you, Amanda. No, wait, let me finish. I know Kincannon's staked a claim. If he's what makes you happy, then I'm glad for you. Just . . . just keep both eyes open concerning

Jesse, okay? And know that if things go sour between you that I'm here for you."

"Conn—"

"Shhh. You don't have to say anything. I just wanted you to know how I felt. And now that I've told you, it's a closed subject." He smiled brightly to reassure her. "Now, you want to tell me what the hell's been going on over here?"

Amanda forced herself to let the subject of Conn's feelings drop. She couldn't deal with one more problem at the moment anyway. When she weighed the implications of confiding in Conn against trying to continue to handle the sabotages alone, the scales tipped heavily in his favor. She didn't want to burden Willie any more than he already was.

And Jesse wasn't there. Her heart lurched painfully as it always did when she thought of him. She needed him. Dammit, where was he?

"Amanda? You want to tell me about it?" Conn asked again softly and with concern. "Maybe I can help."

Forcing her thoughts away from Jesse, she looked uncertainly at Conn.

"Come on, kid. These shoulders are broad for a reason. Take advantage."

She ran a hand through her hair, then in slow, deliberate detail, filled him in.

"Christ," he muttered when she'd finished. "You have any idea who's behind it all?"

"If I had the answer to that one, it wouldn't have gotten this far."

"So what are you doing about it?"

She shook her head. "Trying to salvage what I can. I've neither the water nor the feed left to support the entire herd until the market gets a little healthier. I'll have to sell off some of the stock before they lose what gain we've already accomplished."

Conn considered her idea. "Market's low right now."

"Tell me about it. The last thing I want to do is sell stock, and if I felt I had any other option, I'd take it."

"You do have an option." He leaned forward, propping his elbows on the table. "You could agree to sell the Flying K."

She closed her eyes tightly. "That's no option."

"I understand the money's out there. Developers are fighting for a piece of the pie. It could be an easy way out for you."

She remained silent.

"I gather the sheriff's office hasn't come up with anything," he went on. "Amanda, honey, you'd better give it some thought. Whoever is doing this seems determined . . . and unstoppable. If that's the case, it's only a matter of time. I hate to see this happening to you. It's too much for you to handle. Too much for old Willie as well."

Thinking of Willie, Amanda felt a cutting pang of guilt. "I have to believe he'd feel even worse if we threw in the towel. Not without a good fight."

"But is it worth it? Why not quit before you forfeit the chance to come out ahead? And before you get hurt."

Lifting her chin stubbornly, she looked Conn square in the eye. "I appreciate your stopping over, but if this advice is going to be attached to your offer to help, I'll pass, thanks just the same."

He looked at her for a long moment, then gave an easy shrug. "You always were a stubborn little snot." When she grinned back at him, he asked, "So when are you rounding 'em up?"

She couldn't stop a harsh laugh from escaping. "Another good question. Half of the boys packed up and moved on at first light. I expect the other half will be gone by the end of the day. It seems they, too, have decided to cut their losses since the Flying K is quickly beginning to look like a losing proposition."

"You're not serious?"

"Oh, I wish I weren't. I can't even blame them. They've got to make a living and from where they sit, the prospects of that happening here are getting slim. Charlie Jenkens came back from town last night with a help wanted poster he'd found in the post office. There's a ranch near Kalispell needing help. I told them they'd better take advantage of the offer and go."

"Well, blondie," Conn said with that grin of his that she'd come to trust as a little girl, "since you're so determined to stick this out for the long haul, the only neighborly thing for me to do would be to help you organize a little cattle drive."

She shook her head, frowning. "I can't ask you to—"

"You didn't ask. I offered. I've got the manpower and the time, so no arguments. Let's just get this show on the road."

"Jesse ain't gonna like this," Willie said several days later. He and Amanda had met for an early morning cup of coffee on the front porch.

Amanda followed the direction of Willie's gaze. Except for Smiling Jake, there wasn't a familiar face or horse on the place. One week ago Conn had moved his men in with a vengeance, determined, it seemed, to do whatever he could to help her. Admittedly, she'd even let him do a little bulldozing in the "calling the shots" department. He was not only helping, he'd taken over. She felt guilty about that, but strangely relieved that some of the weight had been lifted from her shoulders. So relieved, she'd even overlooked some of Conn's decisions that she didn't fully agree with.

"Nope, Jesse ain't gonna like it one bit," Willie repeated, chomping down hard on his toothpick.

"Jesse isn't here," she said. Hearing the wounded anger in her own voice, Amanda smiled weakly at Willie. "He isn't here, Willie, and I'm beginning to wonder if he's ever coming back."

Willie just snorted and cast a furtive glance toward the driveway. In that moment, Amanda knew he was thinking the same thing.

Willie's weathered face lost its worried look later that day when a big wind brought Jesse and his Porsche back to the Flying K.

In his typical understated manner, Willie simply nodded as Jesse, red-eyed from lack of sleep and badly in need of a shave, crawled stiffly out of the car.

"How's it going, Willie?" Jesse asked, looking toward the house for a glimpse of Amanda.

"It ain't, and if you'd take a look around instead of sniffin' the air for a scent of that mare you left behind, you'd realize another stud's moved in and staked a claim."

Instantly alert, Jesse took stock of the changes around him. The first thing he spotted was Conn Warren's pickup parked down by the corral. He swore under his breath. "Let's hear it," he said with forced calm.

Willie was all too happy to fill him in. When he'd finished, Jesse strode in grim silence toward the barn.

"Ain't gonna find 'em down there," Willie said.

Jesse stopped cold.

"They're up at the big house . . . in conference."

Matching his stride to the jackhammer beat of his heart, Jesse altered his course toward the house. "What the hell do you find so damn funny?" he asked, aware of Willie's broad grin as the older man struggled to keep pace beside him.

"Nothin'," Willie said.

"Then wipe that stupid smirk off your face."

"Can't help it, Jess. Thinkin' about what you're gonna do to Conn is the first thing I've had to smile about in days."

Amanda was bone tired. It was the only excuse she could think of for falling asleep in the middle of the day. She'd willingly followed Conn's suggestion that she stretch out on the couch in the den while he looked over the books to see if he could come up with any solutions to her current financial dilemma. Prudence should have dictated that her books were none of Conn's business, no matter how helpful he'd become. Prudence had little impact on the hollow, aching loneliness she felt in Jesse's absence, though.

She had drifted off thinking of him. Until she heard his voice raised in anger, she thought she'd merely been dreaming of him again.

". . . out of my house, Warren."

Amanda opened her eyes slowly to see Jesse standing in front of the desk facing Conn.

"Jesse," she cried, bolting up and brushing the hair back from her face. Elation, relief, and unadulterated joy swelled within her, until he looked over his shoulder and met her gaze. His hair was longer than ever, his usually clean-shaven face darkened by a thick stubble of beard. His eyes were hard and accusing, and red-rimmed with fatigue and anger.

He looked awful. He looked wonderful. He looked like he wanted to strangle her.

Before she could say another word, he dismissed her with an I'll-deal-with-you-later glare and turned back to Conn.

Conn had risen from the desk chair. "Hey, Jesse. Glad to see you're back. I was just—"

"—leaving," Jesse broke in, making no attempt to hide his hostility.

Amanda's gaze flew from Jesse's back to Conn's face. The tension crackling between the two men was as fierce as lightning.

"Jesse," she began with the intent of smoothing the waters.

"It's okay, Amanda," Conn said quickly. He met Jesse's cold stare with one of his own before shifting his gaze to Amanda. He smiled as if to reassure her, then faced Jesse again. "Whatever you say, Jesse," he said stiffly, and raised his hands in a gesture of peace. "Just trying to help out until you returned."

"Just trying to help yourself, you mean," Jesse said.

"Jesse!" Amanda exclaimed. "You don't know what you're saying. Conn has been a perfect—"

"Save it, Amanda. Conn's a big boy. He can speak for himself."

Recoiling from the rancor in his tone, Amanda could only stare.

"You always were a hothead, Kincannon," Conn said as he rounded the desk and headed for the door.

"Stay away from what's mine, Warren," Jesse warned, meeting him nose-to-nose when Conn would have walked past him.

Conn stopped and faced him squarely. "It's nice to know there are still some things about you a man can count on, Jesse. You still like to stake your claim on things, on people, don't you? Well, there's another thing about you I'm willing to bank on." He paused, looked directly at Amanda, then back at Jesse. "When you get tired of something, you simply walk away from it. I can wait for that to happen again. Some things are worth waiting for."

Tipping his hat to Amanda, Conn strode out the door.

Amanda felt like she was stalled on a carnival ride. Her stomach somersaulted as she sat there, unable to move. She didn't know what she wanted to do first—launch herself into Jesse's arms and let him kiss her senseless, or rage at him for treating her and Conn like criminals! Conn. Oh, Lord. Someone owed him an apology. The look in Jesse's eyes told her it wouldn't be coming from him.

That same look finally spurred her into action. She'd never seen him this angry and didn't want to stick around to find out what was going to happen.

She bolted around him and headed for the door, intending to stop Conn and at least thank him for all he'd done.

Jesse had other plans for her.

He snagged her arm and whirled her around to face him. "You could induce a peaceful man to violence, Sunshine," he said in a gravelly voice filled with angry heat.

"Jesse—"

"Quiet. All I want from you for the next eight hours is quiet." He urged her out of the room and down the hall.

"Where are you taking me?"

"To bed, Sunshine. *My* bed. Where you belong."

"Jesse, I—"

"Shut up, Amanda, I mean it." He tugged her into his bedroom and slammed the door shut.

"I haven't slept in over twenty-four hours," he added, making quick work of his shirt and boots, "and I'm feelin' about as mean as a wounded grizzly.

"No," he barked when she opened her mouth to speak. "Don't say anything. If I get any madder at you than I am right now, I won't be held responsible for what I do."

With that, he collapsed on the bed and pulled her down with him. Folding her tightly in his arms, he kissed her, long and deep and hard. Then he threw an arm and a leg over her to hold her down and promptly fell asleep.

Stunned, shaken, and happier than she'd been since he left her, Amanda gave in to her own fatigue and let his deep, heavy breathing lull her into her own much-needed sleep.

When she awoke, it was to a shadowy darkness outside the window and the silken warmth of Jesse's mouth on her breast.

She threaded her hands through his hair. "If this is a dream, please don't wake me up."

"One of us," he whispered, finishing with the buttons on her shirt and tugging it off her shoulders, "is overdressed for this occasion."

She arched up to help him with her undershirt, then groaned when he rubbed his bearded jaw against a taut nipple. "One of us is sporting a little more than peach fuzz."

His head came up; his hand rose to his jaw. "Oh, baby, I'm sorry, I forgot. I'll go shave."

"No!" She stopped him with a hand on his cheek and guided his mouth back to her breast. "No. I don't want you going anywhere. Besides, it feels . . . interesting."

Jesse's chuckle was deep and irreverent as he polished her breast with his tongue, then moved with studied languor down her body. "I'll show you interesting," he muttered, tugging on the waistband of her jeans with his teeth. "Just as soon as I get you out of these damn pants."

He showed her more than interesting. He showed her heaven and a little glimpse of hell as with his mouth and hands he lured her to the edge of sensation and back, again and again, allowing both of them their ecstasy. When it was over and she lay breathless and trembling beside him, all she could think about was the next time he would take her there.

"Don't go back to sleep on me, Sunshine. I want to talk with you." Jesse rolled her from her back to her side so she was facing him. Wedging one knee between her long, silken thighs, he drew her against him. Feeling her wince, he gazed at her with concern.

"Baby, did I hurt you?"

"No, no. I'm a little tender, that's all."

"Here?" With gentle fingers he probed the inside of her thigh.

"Mmmm," she murmured drowsily. "It's okay. Just a little . . . ah . . ." She faltered, and he could tell by the way she burrowed her face against his neck that she was embarrassed.

"Whisker burn?" he asked, when he realized the source of her discomfort.

She nodded.

Filled with love and desire and not nearly enough guilt, Jesse suppressed a chuckle and tucked her head under his chin. He drew her closer. "Lord, I missed you."

In his entire life, he couldn't remember missing anyone more than he'd missed the woman falling asleep in his arms. Not the mother he'd never known, not the father who'd written him off at birth, not the dozen women who'd been drawn to his outlaw looks and bad-boy reputation. He'd never before felt that gut-clenching ache of loneliness so acutely. Only Amanda, who'd fought her attraction at every turn, who'd run like a rabbit from the fox, could soothe the hollow, all-consuming pain he'd felt when he left her.

"Are you still angry with me?" she asked, her voice

so soft and hesitant, he could tell she was no longer
fighting sleep.

He stared into the darkness, running his hand up
and down her back. "I was never angry with you. With
circumstances, yes. With the fact that I'd had to leave
you to face what you did alone. That Warren had
wormed his way into your confidence.

"He only helped me, Jess."

"I know, baby. I owe him an apology. If I have to eat
some crow to accomplish it, I promise I'll deliver it."

He waited then for the question she had every right
in hell to ask. He owed her an explanation for where
he'd been, what he'd been doing. She deserved an
answer. But she didn't ask, and by not doing so, he
knew what she was trying to tell him.

She was offering him her trust. Complete, uncategorical trust. It was a gift so great, it made him
speechless. So special it humbled him. So unexpected, he didn't know how to return the gesture.

She must have sensed his uncertainty and decided
to make it go away.

"Did you have a good flight back home?" she asked.

Small talk, he thought. What a woman. For the
first time in his life he had the unqualified trust of a
woman he loved, and an insecurity held over from
adolescence was making him bungle the job like a cat
burglar wearing handcuffs. But this woman, this
wispy little blonde who could pack a pair of faded
denims better than any woman he'd ever known, was
taking him by the hand and leading him away from
the source of his discomfort. With small talk.

He hugged her hard and accepted her offering like
a sinner stealing from the collection plate. "There
was no flight."

After a moment of confusion she asked skeptically,
"You drove? From Tennessee?"

"Um-hmm."

"But that must have taken days."

"Several."

"Why didn't you just fly?"

"Promise you'll still love me?"

She nodded.

"I don't do planes, Sunshine."

She mulled that over for a while, then he felt her grin against his neck. "You're afraid of flying," she said.

He could tell that the idea of this big, supposedly tough cowboy being scared witless at the thought of leaving the ground tickled the hell out of her.

"If you laugh," he warned, hearing the laughter in his own voice, "it'll go real hard on you."

"Is that a threat or a promise?" she asked with a giggle, getting into the spirit of things.

In answer, he grabbed her hand and guided it down between their bodies. When she closed her small fist around him, he groaned and swelled in her hand.

"I just love a man who makes good on his promises," she murmured.

He rolled her swiftly to her back, pinning her arms above her head with one hand. With the other, he parted her thighs. "And I love a woman who recognizes a threat when she hears one." He watched her eyes go all smoky and dark as he sank deep inside her. "You're in trouble now, Sunshine. Deep, dark trouble."

"I cut my teeth on trouble," she replied with what he decided to interpret as a greedy sigh. "Trouble is my middle name. Trouble and I go way back. Trouble—"

"Amanda," he interrupted, matching his breathing to his long, full strokes.

"Hmmm?"

"I get the picture, darlin'. And I'm prepared to give you all the trouble you can handle."

"And," she reminded him, moaning as she stretched and shivered and wrapped her slim legs around him, "you always make good on your promises."

"Always," he whispered, and closed his mouth over hers. "Always . . ."

Ten

If the sky had ever been bluer, Amanda couldn't remember the day. Sunlight fairly spilled across the landscape, painting everything burnished gold. It kissed the tips of the not-so-distant mountaintops, then ricocheted across the valley to warm Amanda's shoulders and cast midnight-blue highlights on Eclipse's glistening black coat. She nudged him gently with her knees and cut a path toward the line shack.

It was Sunday, rest day. She didn't feel like resting, though. She felt restless and eager. After two weeks of uncertain waiting, Jesse was finally back. She told herself it didn't matter that he hadn't confided in her about where he'd been. It didn't matter that in the middle of the night he had, for the first time, pressed her to consider selling. What mattered was that he'd come home.

Smiling at the memory of the previous night's lovemaking, she coaxed Eclipse into a ground-swallowing gallop. The sooner she reached the line shack, the sooner she'd see Jesse again.

He'd risen early and let her sleep late. She'd been a

little surprised he'd left her alone without Willie to play protector. Surprised and delighted. Even during Jesse's absence the past two weeks, Willie had practically camped outside her bedroom door each night. This was the first taste of freedom she'd had since the barn fire. She welcomed the solitude.

But not for long. She missed Jesse.

After a quick cup of coffee, she'd gone looking for him. She'd found the barn deserted and a note tacked to Eclipse's stall. *Meet me at the line shack, noon. Jesse.*

She'd felt her body quicken with latent, sensual response as she remembered the lusty afternoon they'd spent at the line shack several weeks ago. Without hesitation, she'd saddled up Eclipse and headed out.

Amazing, she thought as she rode south, that after last night's passion-filled reunion, she could want him so desperately again. She was filled with a shimmering anticipation, a splintering excitement. She sensed that Eclipse felt it, too, as she reined the sturdy stallion down into an arroyo and up the opposite bank.

It was Jesse's fault she felt this way, she decided. Jesse's special brand of magic. Only he could make her forget the problems with the ranch. And if only for this one day, she was determined not to think about fires or finances or disappearing cattle. Or the danger she could possibly be in.

Forcefully shoving away the unease that accompanied that last thought, she gave Eclipse his head and hung on as he picked his way up the steep slope, then down the other side.

The line shack sat alone among the rock and smatterings of prairie grass. Storm-battered and sun-baked, the ancient but sturdy structure had been refuge and camp to countless cowhands over the years.

Amanda reined in and looked around. Jesse's horse was nowhere in sight. The place appeared to be deserted, even though there were hoofprints in the dust by the door.

As an unsettling chill inched up her spine, she looked again for signs of life. She spotted no one. Nothing. One of the hands must have ridden by recently, she decided, though she was stung by an uncomfortable feeling that something wasn't quite right.

"You're getting paranoid, Carter," she muttered to herself. No doubt it was because she was used to Jesse or Willie dogging her tracks every moment of the day. This newfound freedom was going to take some getting used to. She laughed, figuring that if she wasn't careful, she'd be· hiding from her own shadow next.

She slipped off Eclipse's back and looped his reins over the hitching post. Deciding to wait for Jesse inside, she climbed the two sagging steps.

The heavy wooden door opened with a little persuasion from her shoulder. After creaking and complaining noisily, it finally gave way. Amanda stood for a moment on the threshold, giving her eyes time to adjust to the diffused light. Then she stepped inside.

After riding for almost an hour under the July sun, she welcomed the cool shadows of the interior of the old wooden building. Or was it the memories she welcomed? And the return of her renegade lover.

She removed her hat, tossing it onto a small, rough-hewn table while her attention riveted on the cot beside it.

The flowers were still there. Her heart did a slow tumble as she looked at them, and remembered.

Dried now and faded, the wildflowers lay in careless disarray over the dark gray blanket. They had been fresh flowers when she'd seen them last, a rainbow of blues and lavenders and honey golds. Jesse had picked them for her, then scattered them over the blanket before he laid her down. She could still smell their wild floral scent, almost feel the springy, yielding freshness of them beneath her as Jesse crushed her to the bed and loved her.

She closed her eyes for a moment to quell the sweet stab of yearning, then began gathering the dried stems and fragrant petals. The sound of heavy, booted footsteps stopped her. Heart racing in anticipation, she held the broken bouquet to her breast and turned to greet Jesse with a smile.

Only she didn't see Jesse. She saw instead a fleeting glimpse of sunlight as the door swung violently shut, throwing the shack into pitch blackness.

It took a heartbeat for her to register what had just happened. It took another before she fully believed it. Startled, confused, she called his name. "Jesse?"

He didn't answer.

Carefully, the flowers still clutched in her hand, she walked the three steps to the door. Pressing her cheek against the wood, she listened, then repeated his name. "Jesse. If this is supposed to be a game, you'd just as well know right now, I don't want to play."

Though she'd tried to sound playful and casual, she heard the breathless unease in her voice. When again she received no response, she felt her first real stirring of fear.

She tried the latch on the door. It wouldn't budge.

"Jesse!" she cried, not even trying to hide her panic. "Jesse, open the door." Her breath caught in her throat and stalled. "This isn't funny anymore!"

For several long, painful heartbeats, she stood there fighting the fear, and tried to deny anything out of the ordinary was happening. But something was happening. And it wasn't ordinary. And whatever it was, it was frightening her.

She threw the flowers to the floor and attacked the door with both hands. It was sealed as tight as a tomb.

Returning footsteps brought her head up. Relief swamped her. But then as fast as they'd come, the footsteps faded. Sound was replaced by scent. Her heart lurched violently as the unmistakable stench of gasoline permeated her senses.

"Oh, God," she whispered, pleading, praying that she was wrong. "Oh, God please . . . please, not fire."

Even before she smelled the smoke seeping in through the cracks in the walls, she knew her prayer was not going to be answered. God wasn't going to get her out of this. She was on her own.

Gathering her wits about her, Amanda felt her way around the dark room. Searching blindly for the shutter-covered window, she stumbled over a footstool and almost went down. The wall with the window in it broke her fall.

She groped for the lock. Like the door, the sash was sealed tight.

Fighting with everything that was in her, she tried to keep calm. Perspiration beaded on her forehead. A hot, sticky trickle of sweat inched its way between her breasts as she listened to the crackle of the fire. It was growing stronger.

Reaching for the stool that had tripped her, she raised it over her head and smashed it hard against the windowpane. Broken glass sprayed wildly. Mindless of the jagged splinters that lined the window casing and sliced into her fingers, she fumbled in the dark for the latch to the shutter.

"Open, damn you!" she raged, unable to accept that her struggle was futile. The shutters were nailed shut from the outside. All avenues of escape had been purposefully blocked.

The fire grew louder. Like a hungry wolf it snarled and raged, lapping greedily at the tinder dry wood. The line shack became hotter with every passing second, the air thicker, the scent more acrid. Breathing was increasingly difficult. She had to get out or she was going to die!

In a frantic dive for the door, she lost her footing and stumbled over the end of the cot. This time nothing broke her fall. She landed on the wood floor with a jarring thud.

Through a shattering explosion of pain, she felt a heavy, stinging sensation thrum to life in her temple. Dazed, disoriented, she raised a hand to her head and felt the hot stickiness of her own blood.

Something . . . she thought vaguely, fighting the growing pain in her head and an unnatural, disabling weakness. . . . *have to do something. Have to . . . have to . . . get out . . .*

Driven by instinct alone, she crawled toward the door, her fingers digging into the wood boards.

All around her the fire roared; the smoke choked and suffocated. Breath-stealing heat engulfed her, sapping her remaining strength until a strange sense of detachment settled over her.

She didn't fight for the consciousness she felt ebbing away. She couldn't. She could only think of Jesse.

With the stench of smoke burning her lungs and the brittle cushion of wildflowers crushed like broken dreams beneath her cheek, Amanda let go and drifted toward the compelling relief of oblivion.

At a few minutes before eleven Jesse roared back into the Flying K's drive. His unannounced morning visit to his sister had been enlightening. Painfully so.

His gut twisted just thinking about it. He wrenched open the car door and shoved himself outside.

How could he have been so blind? So stupid. He strode toward the house, fighting the rage that threatened to shove him over the edge. Anger as black as onyx was all tangled up with love for his sister, with shame for what she'd tried to do, and with the grim realization that he would have to tell Amanda.

Willie was beside him before he hit the front porch steps.

"What's up, Jess?"

Jesse clenched his jaw against an emotion so raw, he didn't know how to deal with it. Willie had suffered, too, at his sister's hands. "Where's Amanda?"

"I thought she was with you."

Jesse stopped and looked at him sharply.

"I thought she was with you, Jess," Willie repeated as a frown creased his brow below his hat brim. "When I didn't see her around and your car was gone, I figured the two of you'd gone off somewhere."

Jesse swore softly under his breath. Some protector he was.

"Jess?"

"It's all right, Willie." Jesse laid a consoling hand on Willie's arm. "I left at first light. I thought she'd sleep in and I'd get back before she got up. I was gone longer than I expected. You haven't seen her?"

Willie shook his head.

"I'll be right back."

He returned when a quick search of the bedroom and a brief visit with Tina told him what he needed to know.

"Come on," he said to Willie, and cleared the porch steps in one long stride. "Let's check the barn."

"She's an independent little cuss, Jesse," Willie said when they discovered Eclipse's stall empty. "Probably just felt like kicking up her heels a mite now that you're back."

Grim-faced, Jesse stepped into the stall and snagged the scrap of paper he'd spotted sticking out of the sawdust.

"Son of a bitch!" he swore, crushing the note in his fist after he'd read the message.

"What's goin' on?"

Jesse checked his watch, then shoved the crumpled ball of paper into Willie's hand.

Willie read the note as Jesse raced for the tack room.

"This ain't your chicken scrawl," Willie said as Jesse sailed back past him with his saddle. He threw it over his gelding's back and jerked the cinch strap tight. The normally calm bay shied and sidestepped, unnerved by Jesse's harsh treatment.

Damning himself for his impatience, Jesse soothed the anxious horse. "She's in trouble, Willie," he said, slipping the bit into the gelding's mouth.

"You want I should call the sheriff?"

"No time." He swung up into the saddle. "Follow me in the pickup. It'll take you longer, but if she's hurt, we may need it."

Without another word, he dug his heels into the snorting bay's flanks. They shot out of the barn at a dead run.

Jesse had made this particular ride dozens of times. Never had it seemed so long. He drove the gelding relentlessly, setting a pace that put them both in danger. Thinking not of the hazards but of Amanda and how he'd failed her, he pressed even harder.

Fear slammed into his gut like a knife when he

crested the final hill and smelled smoke. That knife twisted as he spotted the flames.

"Amanda!" he yelled, charging down the steep, rocky incline with breakneck recklessness. When he was within twenty yards of the burning line shack, he threw himself out of the saddle. He hit the ground running, vaguely aware that Amanda's old stallion pranced nervously nearby.

Roaring like a wounded lion, he attacked the door at full speed, slamming his shoulder into the burning wood like a battering ram.

The blackened wood splintered and gave. Jesse tumbled headlong into the smoke-choked interior.

A low primal groan escaped him when he spotted her lying on the floor.

He scooped her into his arms. Shielding her body with his own, he carried her limp form through the flame-shrouded door and into the sunlight. Fighting the impulse to crush her against him and will her to absorb his lifeblood, he laid her gently on the ground.

She was so still, his own heart balked at beating. She was so pale, he feared his hands would bruise her. But she was already bruised. Bruised and battered and broken.

Behind the shadow of a boulder, he offered a prayer laced with threat, then placed trembling fingers to the vein at her throat. His heart leaped when he felt a faint pulsebeat. Bending over her, he checked her respiration. It was shallow and weak. Not a good sign. And Lord, there was so much blood!

Head wounds, he reminded himself, forcing calm, appeared to bleed more than others. It didn't necessarily mean she'd lost a lot of blood. And she wasn't bleeding now. At least not profusely. Popping the snaps on his shirt, he quickly shrugged it off, then ripped off a sleeve. After knotting it gently but securely around her head, he checked for other injuries.

She groaned in pain when he found a sore spot. Her kittenish whimper fostered both anguish and hope within him. The fact that she responded at all had to be a good sign.

"Sunshine," he whispered, cradling her against him when she moaned again. "Hang on, sweetheart. Just hang on. You're going to be all right.

"Willie," he muttered under his breath, listening for the sound of the truck. "Hurry, man."

Amanda awoke to stark, sterile white. She tried to close her eyes against a bright, piercing light that attacked her senses as angrily as the cavelike blackness of her nightmare. And then she remembered. It hadn't been a nightmare. It had been real. As real as the fear that still shadowed her. As real as the pain she was feeling. She hadn't planned on pain after death. She didn't like it.

"Easy, Miss Carter," a voice said. "I know this is uncomfortable, but bear with me a little longer. We'll have you feeling better in no time."

She wasn't dead? That would explain why she hurt so much.

"I'm almost through, then you can go back to sleep, okay?"

She tried to say no. It wasn't okay. She wanted to be left alone. But the words didn't come. Damning the weakness that wouldn't let her defend herself, she gave in and lay still for the cold hands that probed her.

"Can you hear me, Miss Carter?"

She must have nodded.

"That's good. Good. Try to relax now. You're doing just fine. You've got a nasty knot on your head but no concussion. You've taken in a lot of smoke, but with a little healing time you'll be feeling just fine. And though I'm sure the cuts on your hands sting like blue blazes, they'll hardly leave any scars.

"Now, hang on a minute and I'll give you a little something to make you more comfortable. Then I'll let them take you to a room, okay?"

Anything. Anything. Just leave me alone. She felt the sharp prick of a needle, then nothing.

Jesse knew, as he skidded the Porsche to a stop, that it had been the longest twenty-four hours of his life. He slammed the car door without a backward glance and headed at a trot toward the hospital, taking the front steps two at a time.

Tina had been right. Reluctant as he'd been to leave Amanda's side for even a few hours that morning, a shower and shave had been a necessity. If not for his sake, then for Amanda's. His eyes red-rimmed and bloodshot from lack of sleep, his clothes still filthy and smelling from the fire, he'd looked as much like a victim as Amanda when he and Willie had brought her into the emergency room the previous afternoon.

The shower wasn't the only thing that had made him feel better. Before he could face Amanda again, he'd had a score to settle.

Pain shot through his knuckles when he punched the elevator button. He flexed his fingers, wondering if any were broken. It didn't matter. That one punch had been worth it. He'd liked to have thrown a few more. He would have, too, if it hadn't been for Sheriff Thompson and his deputy.

Eager to see Amanda and tell her, her problems were over, he slipped out of the elevator and strode down the hall toward her room. A combination of adrenaline and gut-clenching fear for her life had kept him wired like no marathon song writing session ever had. But the adrenaline rush was wearing off, and for the past few hours, he'd been running on sheer determination.

The doctors had assured him Amanda would be all right. Still, he'd been scared out of his mind that she wouldn't make it.

The only thing keeping him on his feet had been the anticipation of seeing her big brown eyes wide open and smiling for him. Sucking in a deep breath, he shoved open the door to room 313.

Relief and elation filled his chest when he saw she was awake. Her eyes were finally open . . . but she wasn't smiling.

He stood there for a suspended moment, absorbing the tension that radiated from her in shattering waves. Then, moving slowly to the foot of the bed, he studied her expression more carefully.

He wanted to blame the look in her eyes on pain. She had to have pain. Just seeing her this way, all bruised and bandaged, made him hurt for her.

"Amanda? Amanda . . . baby, what is it?"

Then he saw Lucy emerge from the shadows behind the door.

Eleven

Amanda had never been more relieved to see anyone in her life. She looked from brother to sister, loving one, fearing the other.

"What are you doing here, Luce?" Jesse asked stoically.

"I've been waiting for the patient to wake up so I could talk to her."

Jesse shifted his shoulders uneasily. "I don't think that's such a good idea. Maybe you'd better just go, okay?"

Amanda watched as the two Kincannons stared at each other for a tense, silent moment. It was Lucy who finally broke eye contact.

"I'll go," she said, glancing at Amanda, "but not before I say what I came to say."

"I'm not sure Amanda's up to hearing anything you have to say," Jesse said, and gazed at Amanda with concern.

"It's okay, Jess," she said. "I'm all right."

"I don't expect you to understand," Lucy began, her straight, pointed chin rising a notch. "And I don't want you to think this is some grand gesture to clear my conscience or put you at ease."

"Lucy," Jesse said warningly.

She glanced at him, then hurried on. "I knew Jesse would never ask me to fight his battles. That's one of the things I love about him. He's proud. Like me." She paused and looked at him again, her hard eyes soft and beseeching. Then her expression became stony again, and she turned her gaze back to a bewildered Amanda.

"That surprises you, doesn't it? That I can speak about love for my brother? Oh, yes, I'm capable of love," she said with a tight, humorless smile. "Only I never got much of a chance to show it, because there was never any love in my life to return. Not until Jesse. He was the only one who ever made me feel important."

Amanda searched Jesse's face for an explanation of what was taking place here. But Jesse, apparently lost in his own private anguish, was looking past her at some point beyond, or was it at some point back?

Lucy drew Amanda's attention again with a voice uncharacteristically filled with emotion. "At first I thought it was my fault my father couldn't love me—"

"Wait." Amanda felt a surge of pity for this harsh, unyielding woman she neither knew nor understood. "I don't think this is anything I need to hear."

"Well, you're going to hear it," Lucy bit back, brushing aside Amanda's show of empathy. "You're going to hear it so you'll know. You need to know that as I grew older, I realized why my father and my mother couldn't love me. It was because of *your* mother. It was her fault. And then yours."

"What are you talking about?" Amanda asked, stunned. "Jesse? What is she talking about?"

"It's really very simple," Lucy said before Jesse could speak. She crossed her arms tightly under her breasts. "Walt couldn't love me because he loved your mother. Every time he looked at me, he wished I were your mother's child, *his* and your mother's."

"That's not true!" Amanda cried. "My mother—"

"Your mother knew how Walt felt about her. My mother knew it, too, and because of it, every time she looked at me, she saw another way she'd failed Walt. That's why she finally had Jesse. She was still clinging to the hope that she could make Walt love her. She died trying to make him love her."

For a moment, Amanda was too shocked to speak. "It wasn't my mother's fault that your parents had problems," she finally managed to say.

"She could have left."

"My father's work was here. What could she do?"

"She could have convinced him to leave! If she was capable of making two men love her, she was capable of anything."

"That's it, Luce," Jesse broke in. "I wouldn't have let it get this far if I'd known where this was headed. Amanda doesn't need to defend her mother to you."

"Then you came along," Lucy continued, railing at Amanda as if she hadn't heard him.

Jesse moved as if to physically remove Lucy from the room, but Amanda stopped him. "No, Jess. Let her go. Let her get it out so we can get on with our lives."

"I used to watch Walt with you," Lucy said, her voice growing quiet and thoughtful. "The way he'd fuss over you like you were his prize possession, his little golden-haired girl. God, I hated you for that. You weren't his child, or even his grandchild, but he treated you like . . ."

"Like what?" Amanda prompted, astounded by what Lucy was saying, fighting stirrings of sympathy for this woman who had turned her life upside down.

"Like he'd never treated me or Jesse," Lucy finished, turning to face Amanda again. She was silent for a long time, then shook her head. "I thought I was rid of you when you finally left for college. But I was wrong, wasn't I? Even after he died Walt made sure little Amanda was taken care of. It was the ultimate insult when he left control of the ranch to you. That's when I decided I'd had enough. I made up my mind I wasn't going to play second fiddle to you again. Only my little ploys to scare you away didn't work, did they?"

Though Lucy's confession did not surprise Amanda, it was still the last thing she had expected. Her gaze strayed to Jesse. He was watching his sister in utter silence. His face was a mask, but his stance revealed the tension and hurt he was working so hard to conceal.

"Jesse had nothing to do with any of this," Lucy said almost smugly. "I had you convinced he did, didn't I?"

Amanda opened her mouth to deny it, but Lucy swept on.

"You are so damn gullible! You believed every lie I told you about Jesse, didn't you? Didn't you? And you let those lies fester and grow until you doubted his every move. You actually thought it was Jesse who trapped you in that burning line shack."

Amanda turned anguished eyes to Jesse and opened her mouth to deny Lucy's accusation. The pain she saw flicker across his face stopped her, though. Did he believe Lucy? Considering how much she had mistrusted him in the beginning, Amanda couldn't blame him if he did. She had to tell him that her last thoughts had been of him, not because she believed he was trying to kill her, but because the thought of never seeing him again was a hundred times more painful than her fear of death.

She started to speak, but Lucy's harsh voice interrupted her. "You make me sick. You don't deserve him. But for some unknown reason, he loves you. And that, sweet Amanda, is why I'm here."

Glaring at Amanda, Lucy stepped closer to the bed. "I'm a lot of things, but one thing I'm not is a user. I don't want Jesse taking the blame for something I was responsible for, at least in part. Jesse is innocent of everything but being fool enough to fall in love with you. It was Conn who did all those things to you, you little fool!"

Amanda's heart shuddered with shocked surprise. "Conn?"

"Yes, damn him." Lucy looked toward the ceiling, visibly shaken. "Look, I never meant for things to go so far. I just wanted to scare you. Just make it hard on you so you'd pack up and leave."

"Why—why Conn?" Amanda asked when she could form the words.

"Because he's a bigger fool than you are. He's gotten himself in real deep on some gambling debts. He agreed to help me when I told him I'd cut him in on the profits from the sale of the Flying K. Only he began to play too rough. I was ready to forget the entire scheme long before he set the barn on fire and forced your car off the road. But he was out of control by then. I begged him to stop. He promised me he would. And for a while, he did. I honestly thought it was over. Then I heard about the grass fires and all the other incidents, and I knew he was at it again. When Jesse came to see me yesterday morning determined to find out if I was behind the trouble, I told him the whole story. And I told him that I was afraid of what Conn would pull next."

Amanda shivered. "And what he pulled next was to lure me out to the line shack and set it on fire. Lord, he must hate me."

"What he hates," Jesse said, "is your rejection of

him. It galled him to no end that you preferred me to him. But more than that, he was fighting for his life. I don't know what or who was after him, but they were leaning on him pretty heavy. He'd already mortgaged his own spread to the hilt. He was counting on the money from the sale of the Flying K to get him out from under."

Amanda squeezed her eyes shut, thinking of all the times Conn had been in the house, of how close she'd let him get to her.

"Don't worry," Jesse assured her. "Conn's been taken care of."

Amanda knew instinctively that Jesse had had a part in whatever had happened to Conn. It was then that she noticed the bandage on his right hand. "Jesse?" she asked tentatively.

He lifted his hand and studied it for a moment. "It'll be sore for a while," he said, then managed a slight smile. "But Conn's jaw probably feels a lot worse."

His smile faded, and he glanced at his sister. "You should probably go now, Lucy."

Lucy gazed at Amanda, then at her brother, with a look that was part pleading, part pathos. Jesse wouldn't, or couldn't, meet her eyes. Amanda felt an acute sympathy for the hard, bitter woman who had, by her trickery and deceit, lost the one person who had ever held a special place in her life. Without another word, Lucy gathered her purse and walked stiffly out of the room.

"I'm so sorry, Jesse," Amanda whispered as tears clouded her eyes.

He forced a grim smile. "You all right?"

She nodded because she couldn't trust herself to speak.

"Will you be all right alone for a while?"

Again, she nodded.

"I've got a little thinking to do, Sunshine."

"It's okay." She averted her eyes so he wouldn't see her pain. So she couldn't see his haunted blue eyes, his dark head bending toward her. He placed a gentle kiss on her forehead, then turned and walked out the door.

Amanda closed her eyes. She closed her mind. At least she tried to.

Jesse had been everything she'd ever wanted. He'd loved her like she'd never thought she could be loved. He'd made a woman of her that she'd never thought she could be. All he'd asked in return was her trust. All she'd given him was doubt, her trust coming much too late.

They released her later that same day. A stone-faced yet fussy Willie drove her home.

"How you feelin', Mandy-girl? Better?"

She couldn't bear to see new lines of tension deepening the grooves in his already-wrinkled face, so she nodded and assured him she was fine.

Only she wasn't fine and she didn't think she would ever be fine again.

Tina welcomed her at the ranch house door with the intent of tucking her into bed. It took Amanda a little talking and a lot of strain to convince the housekeeper she wanted to recuperate in the fore-man's cottage. She couldn't stay at the big house. There were too many memories there. Memories that hurt and haunted and turned a sweet aching need into hollow, empty despair.

Between short and fitful periods of restless sleep throughout the day, she schooled herself to block the memory of Jesse's face when he'd left her room. She didn't want to think about the pain she'd seen in his eyes.

After darkness came and she'd seen no sign of him,

she shed all the tears she had left inside her. Soul-bleeding, heart-rending tears, until she was drained dry of pain and emotion. Jesse was a proud man. He'd suffered a greater loss than she had. He'd lost the bond between a brother and a sister . . . and believed he'd lost the trust of the woman he loved. Where was he so that she could tell him the truth?

Drifting in and out of sleep that late, lost midnight, Amanda awoke to a dream that was more sound than picture. More feeling than substance. It was a sound so sweet, she felt it flutter like a summer breeze straight to her heart, so vivid, she wanted to cry because it was only a dream.

In the dream Jesse was playing for her, singing for her . . . like that first night she'd gone to him and he'd teased her and flirted with her and kissed her in the moonlight on the patio.

Not wanting to let it go, she burrowed deeper into her bed, clinging to the mellow strains of his guitar as his music floated through the night and into her bedroom window.

Awareness, so stunning, it sent her heart tripping and so wonderful, it brought hope leaping, sat her straight up in bed. She listened, then heard it again.

Instantly awake, she flew out of bed and over to the window. Moonlight spilled through the darkness, cutting a path to the big house where Jesse—a flesh-and-blood Jesse—sat on the patio alone. He was playing for her. Singing for her. Beckoning her to come.

The last time she'd run across the same path, the grass had been dewy wet and springtime cool beneath her bare feet. As fast as her recent injuries allowed, she raced across the path again, carelessly knotting the belt of her kimono, not noticing that the hard-packed earth and brittle, summer-dried grass bit at the soles of her feet.

Holding her hair from her eyes and her breath in check, she stopped in the shadows of the lilacs and took her fill of him.

He looked every bit the outlaw . . . his midnight-black hair was still too long, the jeans he wore low on his hips too tight. He was the same irreverent sinner she'd been afraid to let into her heart. And she wanted to touch him so bad, it hurt.

If he didn't see her soon or say something, she was going to die of sheer desperation!

"Still sneaking around in the bushes, I see." His soft, drawling voice heated her blood and sent her pulse racing. "Old habits are hard to break, huh, Sunshine?"

With her chest full of want, her heart full of love, she slipped out of the darkness and into the moonlight.

Jesse stilled his guitar.

Her heart stilled, too, as he looked at her.

"Jess," she whispered.

He stopped her with a shake of his head. "Don't talk. Not yet." Holding her gaze with his own, he set aside his guitar and extended his hand. "Come. I just need to hold you."

She flew onto his lap and into his arms. Arms that welcomed and enfolded and held her until the ache inside her eased away.

He threaded his fingers through her hair, touched the small, white bandage on her temple, then framed her face in his hands. His eyes were a clear, stunning blue as he studied her mouth, her eyes, and then as if he couldn't help it, her mouth again.

"I thought I'd lost you, Sunshine," he whispered, brushing away the tears that tracked down her cheeks.

Touching his lips to hers as if she were a fragile, crushable flower, he kissed her again and again, punctuating each loving kiss with a lingering look of concern.

The kisses grew longer, stronger, until the hurt and the hunger stole the gentleness from his mouth and the breath from her body. Amanda clung to him, returning his passion with each beat of her heart.

When they'd tasted and feasted and reassured themselves that their reunion was real, they gentled their kisses, mellowed their loving to silken whispers and tender sighs.

There were words that needed to be spoken. Hurts that needed to be healed. But the silence stretched and lengthened as they sat as close as two people could sit, each waiting for the right words to come.

Jesse took the first step. Pressing her cheek to his chest, he rested his chin on the top of her head. "Tina tells me you didn't eat your supper," he said, his tone laced with concern.

Amanda ran a hand over his lean belly, reacquainting herself with the feel of him, the strength of him, the warmth. "I wasn't hungry."

But hunger wasn't the issue, their future was. Yet again, the quiet settled until Jesse growled and hugged her tight. "Lord, we're a pair, aren't we? There's so much I want to say to you, but I get this ridiculous feeling that next we'll be talking about the weather."

"Partly cloudy. Chance of rain," she said, letting him know she was as uncertain as he was. Pulling away so she could see his face, she touched a hand to his cheek. "Jesse, Lucy was wrong. For a moment, when the door first shut and I smelled the gasoline, I did think it was you, but only because you were supposed to be there. But when he set the fire, I knew it couldn't be you. You would never—" Her voice broke on a sob.

"Shhh," he whispered. "I know you didn't really think it was me. I didn't believe Lucy."

"But you looked so pained, as if you did believe her."

"If I looked pained, it was because of my own guilt." He paused to stroke her hair. "I placed some boulder-sized expectations on you, Amanda, then ran like a scalded dog when you buckled under the load. No," he said, stopping her when she would have spoken. "Let me finish."

Looking deep into her eyes, he spoke straight from his heart. "You're the best thing that's ever happened to me, Amanda, and at the first sign of doubt on your part, I was ready to throw away what we had."

He pulled her against him again and held her close. "You gave me so much. You'll never know what it meant to me when I came back from Tennessee and you didn't ask where I'd been, what I'd been doing. You had every right to, yet you didn't question. It blew me away. It was the best gift anyone had ever given me and I wallowed in it. I even went so far as to rationalize that if I explained what I'd been up to, it would somehow minimize what you'd done. But I was wrong. Selfish and wrong. Blind trust is for fools and schemers. You're neither."

He shook his head in self-disgust. "It's no wonder you thought at first I was responsible for everything that had happened to you. You didn't know anything about me. And the part that really fries me is that I was constantly testing you. I was purposefully eva-sive. I didn't want you to know what I did for a living, where I lived, who I was. I kept telling myself that I deserved that trust from you, and the more you gave it, the more I pushed, until I got exactly what I deserved. And you deserved so much better."

Her heart tripped with hope. "All I want is you,

Jess. You're all I've ever wanted. And I know everything about you that I need to know."

"You don't know," he murmured. "But I want to tell you."

And since it seemed so important to him, she listened in stunned silence while he did. Jesse, it seemed, didn't just write a song when he needed a buck. From what she could gather from his modest, unembellished account, he was one of the hottest properties in the country-western business. By reading between the lines, she also gathered that Jesse was at least half of the reason Hoyt Haggerty was still top dog on the country charts. Jesse and Hoyt had teamed up almost eight years ago. The combination of Jesse's music and Hoyt's voice had made both of them rich.

"Rich?" Amanda echoed, caught up in the wonder of it all.

For the first time, Jesse chuckled. "Let me put it this way. If I never put pen to paper again, we could live in decadent luxury off the copyrights I've sold and the royalties."

All of that explained so much, Amanda mused. The expensive car. His lack of concern about money. The apparent absence of a steady job. He even told her what he'd been doing in Tennessee when he'd left so unexpectedly. Hoyt had been putting the finishing touches on a new album, and he'd needed Jesse's help to iron out a problem with the final cut.

"And just so you know I'm in this for the long haul," Jesse finished, "I managed to hire the men back, order a couple of semiloads of hay for winter feed, and make arrangements for water to be hauled in until the toxins seep out of the reservoir. Oh, and I called that rancher in Bozeman to have that new bull you've been wanting shipped down. He should be here tomorrow morning."

Stunned by his revelations and by all that he'd done for her, she snuggled closer in his arms and held him tight.

"And just so you know, Kincannon, even before this glorious unveiling of your secret life and past, I've always known everything I ever needed to know about you. I've known that you were loving and vulnerable and kind. Jesse . . ." She framed his cheeks in her bandaged fingers and forced him to look at her. "Listen to me. I love you. I loved you when I thought you were a drifter and an outlaw who didn't give a damn about commitment and didn't have a dime to his name."

He searched her eyes, evidently finding what he wanted there, and grinned. "So, now that you know I'm respectable, do you still want anything to do with me?"

She lovingly smoothed the hair from his brow, absorbed in and inspired by his devil blue eyes and outlaw grin. "You'll never be respectable. Not to me. You'll always be my reckless, renegade Jesse."

"Renegade?" He laughed, loving the look in her eyes.

"Renegade."

"I don't want to burst your bubble, Sunshine, but you're looking at a classic case of a domesticated man."

She shook her head. "Never."

He kissed her then. Deeply. Sweetly. "What's it going to take to convince you that this old renegade wants to settle down and make an honest woman out of you?"

Her heart soared, glided, then settled like a golden sunset. "Convince me later," she whispered, and with a secret smile, rose from his lap and tugged him toward the patio door. "Right now, I don't want you settled down. I just want you."

With a grin that was at once winsome and wicked, he followed her lead.

In the darkness of the blue bedroom Jesse laid her down. Moonlight winked over the big four-poster where he proceeded to give her love, goodness, and all the trouble she would ever need.

THE EDITOR'S CORNER

For the best in summertime reading, look no further than the six superb LOVESWEPTs coming your way. As temperatures soar, what better way is there to escape from it all than by enjoying these upcoming love stories?

Barbara Boswell's newest LOVESWEPT is guaranteed to sweep you away into the marvelous world of high romance. A hell raiser from the wrong side of the tracks, Caleb Strong is back, and no red-blooded woman can blame Cheyenne Whitney Merit for giving in to his STRONG TEMPTATION, LOVESWEPT #486. The bad boy who left town years ago has grown into one virile hunk, and his hot, hungry kisses make "good girl" Cheyenne go wild with longing. But just as Caleb burns with desire for Cheyenne, so is he consumed by the need for revenge. And only her tender, healing love can drive away the darkness that threatens their fragile bond. A dramatic, thrilling story that's sensuously charged with unlimited passion.

The hero and heroine in SIZZLE by Marcia Evanick, LOVESWEPT #487, make the most unlikely couple you'll ever meet, but as Eben James and Summer Hudson find out, differences add spice to life . . . and love. Eben keeps his feet firmly planted in the ground, so when he discovers his golden-haired neighbor believes in a legendary sea monster, he's sure the gods are playing a joke on him. But there's nothing laughable about the excitement that crackles on the air whenever their gazes meet. Throwing caution to the wind, he woos Summer, and their courtship, at once uproarious and touching, will have you believing in the sheer magic of romance.

Welcome back Joan J. Domning, who presents the stormy tale of love lost, then regained, in RAINY DAY MAN, LOVESWEPT #488. Shane Halloran was trouble with a capital *T* when Merle Pierce fell hard for him in high school, but she never believed the sexy daredevil would abandon her. She devoted herself to her teenage advice column and tried to forget the man who ruined her for others. Now, more than twenty years later, fate intervenes, and Shane learns a truth Merle would have done anything to hide from him. Tempers flare but are doused in the sea of their long-suppressed passion for each other. Rest assured that all is forgiven between these two when the happy ending comes!

With her spellbinding sensuality, well-loved author Helen Mittermeyer captures A MOMENT IN TIME, LOVESWEPT #489. Hawk Dyhart acts like the consummate hero when he bravely rushes into the ocean to save a swimmer from a shark. Never mind that the shark turns out to be a diving flag and the swimmer an astonishingly beautiful woman who's furious at being rescued. Bahira Massoud is a magnificently exotic creature that Hawk must possess, but Bahira knows too well the danger of surrendering to a master of seduction. Still, she aches to taste the desire that Hawk arouses in her, and Hawk must walk a fine line to capture this sea goddess in his arms. Stunning and breathtaking, this is a romance you can't let yourself miss.

Let Victoria Leigh tantalize you with LITTLE SECRETS, LOVESWEPT #490. Ex-spy turned successful novelist I. J. Carlson drives Cassandra Lockland mad with his mocking glances and wicked come-ons. How could she be attracted to a man who provokes her each time they meet? Carlson sees the fire beneath her cool facade and stokes it with kisses that transform the love scenes in his books into sizzling reality. Once he breaches her defenses and uncovers her hidden fears, he sets out on a glorious campaign to win her trust. Will she be brave enough to face the risk of loving again? You'll be thoroughly mesmerized by this gem of a book.

Mary Kay McComas certainly lands her hero and heroine in a comedy of errors in ASKING FOR TROUBLE, LOVESWEPT #491. It all starts when Sydney Wiesman chooses Tom Ghorman from the contestants offered by the television show *Electra-Love*. He's smart, romantic, funny—the perfect man for the perfect date—but their evening together is filled with one disaster after another. Tom courageously sees them through each time trouble intervenes, but he knows this woman of his dreams can never accept the one thing in his life he can't change. Sydney must leave the safe and boring path to find the greatest adventure of all—a future with Tom. Don't miss this delectable treat.

FANFARE presents four truly spectacular books in women's popular fiction next month. Ask your bookseller for TEXAS! CHASE, the next sizzling novel in the TEXAS! trilogy by bestselling author Sandra Brown, THE MATCHMAKER by critically acclaimed Kay Hooper, RAINBOW by the very talented Patricia Potter, and FOLLOW THE SUN by ever-popular Deborah Smith.

Enjoy the summer with perfect reading from LOVESWEPT and FANFARE!

With every good wish,

Carolyn Nichols

Carolyn Nichols
Editor
LOVESWEPT
Bantam Books
666 Fifth Avenue
New York, NY 10103

THE LATEST IN BOOKS
AND AUDIO CASSETTES

NEW!
Handsome Book Covers Specially Designed To Fit Loveswept Books

Our new French Calf Vinyl book covers come in a set of three great colors—royal blue, scarlet red and kachina green.

Each 7" × 9½" book cover has two deep vertical pockets, a handy sewn-in bookmark, and is soil and scratch resistant.

To order your set, use the form below.

ORDER FORM